Praise for
Becoming Carly Klein

"In *Becoming Carly Klein*, Elizabeth Harlan has given us a heart-warming adventure of a young girl coming of age in 1980s New York City. Not only Carly but her mom and dad as well grow up through this lively and engaging tale of family strife, first love, youthful rebellion, deception, heartbreak, and healing."

—SENATOR CONNIE MACK,
United States Senate 1989–2001,
author of *Citizen Mack: Politics, an Honorable Calling*

"As I reflected upon this beautiful, hilarious, heartrending, truthful, and captivating work, two words finally came to me: a marvel."

—J. L. LOGAN,
Literature Bibliographer, Princeton University

"In *Becoming Carly Klein*, Elizabeth Harlan vividly portrays the gripping and emotionally charged coming-of-age journey of an Upper East Side teenage girl in 1980s New York. As Carly forges her path to self-discovery, she is captivated by love, only to face a betrayal that tests her resolve. Through the trials of heartbreak and the struggle for reconciliation, she unearths her inner strength and resilience, proving that even in the face of adversity, the human spirit has the power to heal and rise anew."

—MARYAM BANIKARIM, cofounder of *NYCNext*
and one of *Fast Company's* "Top 10 Disrupters"

"Under Harlan's brilliant and deft touch, *Becoming Carly Klein* is a fearless exploration of how stepping in the wrong direction can help us step into ourselves. Perceptive and engrossing, this coming-of-age story is an anthem for an under-parented generation, and a reminder that growing up can happen at any age . . . in all its funny, heartbreaking, and messy glory! A deeply satisfying read and one not to miss."

—MARY PASCUAL,
author of *The Byways* and *Walk the Web Lightly*

"As much as her plot and characters, it's Elizabeth Harlan's spare, elegant way with words that gives Carly's story its power to engage a reader of any age, gender, or station."

—BROOKE KROEGER, author of *Undaunted*

"I just adored this book for its psychological depth, its moral complexity, and Harlan's writing skill. It's full of pep but so much more sophisticated and insightful than the usual YA. Harlan is brilliant at showing us the geography of the mother-daughter relationship. A profoundly interesting coming-of-age story. This is your next great read!"

—NEROLI LACEY, author of *The Perfumer's Secret*

"If Holden Caulfield had a great-grandchild, it might be Carly Klein. J. D. Salinger used Holden as narrator to animate his novel; Elizabeth Harlan uses her powers of vivid observation. This will be a riveting read for many teenagers—and a meaningful cautionary tale for their parents."

—GLENN KRAMON, former assistant managing editor
at *The New York Times*

BECOMING
CARLY
KLEIN

BECOMING
CARLY
KLEIN

A Novel

ELIZABETH HARLAN

SPARKPRESS

Published by SparkPress, a BookSparks imprint,
A division of SparkPoint Studio, LLC
Phoenix, Arizona, USA, 85007
www.gosparkpress.com

Published 2024
Printed in the United States of America

Print ISBN: 978-1-68463-266-4
E-ISBN: 978-1-68463-267-1
Library of Congress Control Number: 2024906082

Interior design and typeset by Katherinne Lloyd, The DESK

For my beloved grandgirls:
Maz, Nonie, Katya, and Lily

CHAPTER ONE

C arly sneaks into her mother's office and lies down on the couch. With her head on one of those paper towel things Gwen leaves on the pillow wedge, she pretends she's a patient revealing her problems. The bump from her ponytail is uncomfortable, so Carly pulls off the scrunchie and spreads out her bushy red hair before settling down again. Her mother teaches at the hospital on Wednesday afternoons and won't be home for another few hours.

Carly is a sophomore at Baxter, a girls school on Seventy-Ninth Street at the East River. Her mother believes girls develop more self-confidence in school in the absence of male competition, but Carly has serious doubts. The kids in her class are snobby and cliquish and, to use her best friend Lauren's expression, "vapid."

Even though Jodie Killingsworth is supposed to be her friend, she told her what Harper Phyffe thinks. That Carly is neurotic and having problems in school because "shrinks' kids are all fucked up." Jodie put air quotes around it to show these were Harper's words, not hers, but why is Jodie hanging out with Harper in the first place?

When Carly lies on the couch, she never knows where the thoughts that pop into her mind come from. It's like a write-your-own adventure in which the wildest ideas are the best. Later she'll catch up on the notebooks Gwen keeps in a filing cabinet—one for each patient—where she records what goes on in the sessions.

Katherine, the Irish housekeeper, is ironing clothes in the kitchen and watching the soaps—her favorite is *Search for Tomorrow* and its saga of the McCleary brothers—in between news flashes on the Iran hostage crisis, which she blames on Jimmy Carter. Unlike the Kleins, who are liberal Democrats, Katherine thinks Ronald Reagan walks on water. She's enormous, gets breathless climbing stairs, and almost never comes up to the office, which is at the back of the Kleins' duplex on East Ninety-Sixth Street. So Carly knows she can lie on the patients' couch without being found out.

The routine started during a snowstorm when Carly was thirteen and snuck into her mother's office and discovered the notebooks. Gwen was at Mount Sinai Hospital, where she's on staff, and called home to say she was covering for a colleague and would be home a few hours late.

Carly's father's office is in Midtown, and when he's not traveling for his work directing advertising campaigns for clients like Folgers coffee and Wisk laundry detergent, he rarely gets home before late at night. Carly sees more of Joel's ads on television than she does of him in person.

At first, Carly would skim her mother's notes for superficial information like patients' names and ages and, of course, any juicy parts where sex was mentioned, but now Carly reads every word. She has practically memorized the case histories of most of the patients. She thinks of the snooping as her own private soap opera and looks forward to each new installment.

Because her mother never discusses her work, Carly has learned not to ask questions. She must be extremely careful not to let on that she has any interest in these people who come and go. Nor that she catches glimpses of them in the crack of the hall door to the office.

Carly's favorite is Daniel, the blind junior at Columbia College who majors in music and plays jazz saxophone. Because he can't see her, sometimes she trails him to the bus stop on Madison Avenue and watches through the window of the pizza shop as he waits with his seeing-eye dog for the bus. No one ever says anything about her not buying pizza, because in her school uniform—plaid skirt, white blouse, blue blazer—she blends in with the usual bunch of kids who hang out there from Nightingale on Ninety-Second Street and the French Lycée on Ninety-Fifth.

Daniel's by far the handsomest, sexiest-looking guy she has ever seen. There's Matt Dillon in the movies, and Carly has a serious daddy crush on Michael Landon from *Little House on the Prairie* on TV, but close-up in real life Daniel's amazingly gorgeous.

Lying on the couch, her eyes still closed, Carly reaches back through time to a memory of being young. The tile is bright white all around, across the floor, and up and down the walls of her parents' bathroom. Carly is tracing the light gray grout lines with her toe while sneaking glances at her mother's naked body in the tub. From the window behind where she sits on the closed toilet, early morning sunlight seeps through the blinds, casting striped shadows across the floor.

Carly is pretending she's an explorer and that Gwen is a lush landscape, an island rising from the sea. Carly watches her limbs lying long and splendid in the soapy foam. Gwen drizzles water from a white washcloth over her soft, shapely breasts and tummy and then covers her grassy mound with the square of wet cloth, like a blanket of fresh snow. A smile plays over her mouth. Her body is near, but her spirit is a speck on the horizon, a million miles away. Her breasts, spongy white buoys with dark pinky-purple centers, bob up and down in the sudsy sea.

Carly asks shyly how come she has so much "nipple part," and Gwen tells her the "areola" gets larger after childbirth. Carly wants to know if hers will, too, but a wave of so many questions wells up within her that she can't speak. Through the telescope of her imagination, she sees her mother dreaming of her father and of last night and their lovemaking. Gwen is washing away the sticky stuff of sex while bathing her beautiful body in the languor of their love.

Carly's thoughts wander back to the present. Her eyes open back on the ceiling's cracks and swirls where paint and plaster have parted ways. An image of Annelies, a tall, skinny patient with long black wavy hair, wafts like the wind through Carly's mind. Annelies, a freshman at Hunter College who makes herself vomit after every meal, also dances with the junior company of the New York City Ballet. She wants to drop out of school and join a ballet company full-time, but her parents want her to stay in college.

It especially rankles Carly that in Annelies's last session she and Gwen discussed Annelies's upcoming birthday. Her parents wanted her to come home to celebrate together as a family, but Annelies decided to stay in New York instead. Carly's sixteenth birthday is coming up this Sunday, and Gwen and Joel are so obsessed with their jobs, they haven't said a word about it.

Carly knows from reading the notebook that Gwen thinks Annelies's making herself vomit is her way of getting back at her controlling mother. Annelies says she does it because she's a dancer and has to stay thin. Carly's not exactly fat but what people call "chubby." She envies Annelies's figure and sometimes imagines what it would be like to trade bodies with her. Carly would love to lose weight, but when she tries to make herself vomit after eating, nothing happens. She figures she wasn't born with anorexic genes.

At the sound of Gwen's footsteps on the stairs, Carly jumps up and rushes to put away the patient records. Well practiced in her routine, she quietly closes the office door and returns to her bedroom just in time to settle down at her desk as though she's doing homework.

"Hi, Carly," Gwen calls from the top of the stairs. "How was your day?"

Before Carly gets a chance to answer, Gwen appears at the door to her bedroom, addressing Carly's back. "Hadn't you better collect your books from the kitchen and get started on some homework?"

When Carly doesn't respond, Gwen pushes the door open far enough to position herself where Carly has to see her.

"By the way, do you know why Ms. Harrington wanted to reach me before?"

"How would I know Ms. Harrington's motives? I'm not her shrink."

"Is there a problem at school, Carly?"

"This is not a therapy session, and I am not one of your patients."

A buzzer sounds in another part of the apartment, and Gwen turns to leave. Carly knows Daniel is her mother's four o'clock patient and that he'll be followed by an older woman named Doris, whose husband died last year in a car accident, and then by a training psychologist from Mount Sinai named Kirsten. That gives Carly three hours before dinner at seven thirty, plenty of time to change out of her school uniform and to follow Daniel to the bus stop when his session ends.

CHAPTER TWO

E ven though it's sixty-five degrees, Carly changes into a heavy black wool sweater layered over a black turtleneck, black tights, and work boots with thick wool socks sticking over the tops. Timing her departure for the end of Daniel's session, she goes downstairs to the kitchen and finds Katherine at the stove preparing dinner. Turning a knob, she lights a match to one of the burners, which makes the sudden implosion of a gas range igniting.

"The blue's the hottest part of the flame," Katherine says without looking up. "If you put a finger there, even near, it'll melt right down."

"I'll be sure to stay out of its way," Carly tells her.

She's accustomed to Katherine's unceasing vigilance about all things dangerous and threatening. Not that she'd ever admit it, but Carly enjoys the age-warped way Katherine relates to her, as though Carly were still the little girl of eight who was so often left in her care. Carly helps herself to a handful of Oreo cookies and some milk and hoists herself up onto the washing machine next to the counter where Katherine is working. While Katherine scrapes carrots, Carly dangles her legs and rhythmically kicks her heels into the front of the machine.

When the carrots are scraped, Katherine begins chopping them. "I've just heard about a lady who died last year in New Jersey who's being elected to sainthood. The lady took care of feeding the poor in an entire neighborhood for some twenty-five years, never asking and never receiving one penny in return."

"How'd she support herself?" Carly asks.

"The Lord knows," Katherine tells her, unperturbed by the dilemma that Carly's question poses. "Where there's a will, there's a way." She gathers handfuls of carrot pennies and places them in a saucepan.

"I bet she's on welfare," Carly says. "Maybe the taxpayers should be elected to sainthood instead." She swings her feet against the machine again, this time a little harder to punctuate the point she's making.

"You just watch them clodhoppers of yours, my lass."

Carly knows Katherine's really more upset by her idealistic bubble about the sainted lady from New Jersey being burst than about her boots knocking against the washing machine.

Even though the Kleins are Jewish, Katherine has always assumed it's her duty to instruct Carly on the fundamentals of Catholicism. Carly separates an Oreo and eats away the white filling before consuming the chocolate wafers.

"Mind you don't eat too many of them cookies, Carly. You don't want to get stout like me. But I'd rather see you with a little flesh on them young bones than skinny as a plucked chicken, like that one that sees your mother."

Carly knows Katherine's talking about Annelies and imagines Gwen greeting her with a plate full of Oreo cookies and a glass of whole milk. This leads to a disconnected thought. Is Annelies's long, dark hair naturally wavy, or does she get it permed?

"Of course, that's not as bad as the young 'uns today that

have no shame," Katherine is saying, and Carly can tell from the way she blushes that she's about to tell one of her good stories.

"Take my granddaughter Colleen's friend. Not yet seventeen, and this here friend goes and gets herself with child. And when she comes home to her mother, you know what she tells her about how it happened? The boyfriend and her, they went and used Saran Wrap, your plain old plastic household wrap. Can you imagine? I tell you, there ain't no shame left in the world."

"So? What happened to her?" Carly asks. "What'd she do?"

"Well, I reason she hit the roof, which is what any self-respecting mother in her place would do!"

"No, I mean the girl," Carly persists. "What'd the girl do? Did she have the baby, or what?"

"What else could she do?" Katherine says as she pops a tray of muffins in the oven. "Seems like the damage was already done."

Carly wants desperately to know if the wrap had holes in it or if it just didn't stick in the right places, but she can't bring herself to ask. Then she sees the time on her orange-and-green Swatch and hops down off the washing machine.

"Gotta go," she tells Katherine. "See ya later."

"Not today," Katherine says. "I'm off in a little bit. The chicken's all prepared, and yer mother asked me to post this note on the fridge when I go."

Carly recognizes her mother's no-nonsense block print writing on the paper Katherine takes out of her apron pocket: CARLY, SET OVEN TO 375 AND START CHICKEN ROASTING AT 6:30.

Katherine tapes the note on the refrigerator, opens the door, and shows Carly the Pyrex pan with a chicken sprinkled with seasoning. "This should cook up in an hour. Mind you don't be late about preheating the oven to give it time."

The shiny place on the wing that looks like goose bumps of yellow grizzle makes Carly gag. She ignores the knapsack with her schoolbooks, still lying on the floor where she left it an hour ago, calls out, "See ya," to Katherine, and goes out the back door.

Checking her Swatch, Carly settles herself against the lobby wall facing the elevator and waits. It's only 4:40, so she knows she has a few minutes before Daniel and the dog come down.

As soon as Carly sees the red light go on, indicating that the elevator has stopped at the twelfth floor, her heart starts banging in her chest. Not until they're out on the street does Carly feel her heart begin to slow down. Daniel, in blue jeans and a light blue shirt rolled up at the sleeves, is walking slowly, holding his dog's harness, heading east on Ninety-Sixth Street toward Madison Avenue. Carly hangs back, pulls out a cigarette, and even though there's no breeze at all, cups her hands reflexively as she lights up.

Once they reach the curb at Madison Avenue, the dog stops with Daniel and waits for the light to change to green. Carly is closer now, but she halts a few paces behind where they're waiting. When the light changes, they step off the curb and cross the street in front of the row of stopped cars and taxis. Carly wonders how Daniel and the dog know where to go and when the light turns from red to green. Are there special signals Daniel sends the dog? And can dogs tell the difference between colors?

When they reach the uptown bus stop on the southeast corner, Daniel and the dog stand waiting. Today Carly decides that instead of going into the pizza shop, she'll wait out on the street. She stares at Daniel's head and imagines him combing his hair, his thick straight golden hair, and wonders if he knows by touch when it falls just right.

A little girl with iridescent pink plastic barrettes in her hair says, "Look, Mommy, a blind dog. Can I pet him?"

Her mother vigorously shakes her head no, crosses her index finger over her lips, and mouths "shhh" at the little girl, who goes over and pets the dog anyway.

"Nice doggy," she says twice, holding her hand out to him before she actually pats his head.

Daniel smiles and tells the girl, "He won't bite. Don't worry."

"Does he have a name?" the girl asks, still patting the dog and looking up at Daniel now.

"Beacon's his name," Daniel tells her.

The girl calls to her mother, "The blind dog's name is Beacon, Mommy, and he doesn't bite."

When the number 4 bus comes, everyone waits while Beacon and Daniel climb on first and walk to a seat in back. While the others board, Carly makes a sudden decision. She drops her cigarette and grinds out the stub on the sidewalk with the toe of her boot, roots around in her pocket for a token, and boards the bus. She walks past the mother and the little girl, who have taken seats at the front, goes to the rear, and sits diagonally across from Daniel and the dog.

Carly can barely believe she's doing this. Suddenly, she feels very free and powerful. She can stare and stare as much as she wants and knows he can't see her staring. She inspects his rosy complexion and his clear, smooth skin, unlike guys her age whose faces are covered with zits. Jared Goldfarb, who lives across the hall in 12C, even has pimples on his neck and ears. She wonders if Daniel reads braille or if someone comes and reads to him— the way her great-aunt Mildred had a reader come when she got that eye disease and couldn't see anymore.

But Daniel's situation is different, Carly knows, because she read in Gwen's notebook that his blindness is "congenital," which means he was born with it. When he first became Gwen's patient, back in his first semester at Columbia, Daniel told a story about when he was a boy of four or five. He was visiting his grandparents and staying overnight for the first time at their home on Lake George. His mother and father had driven him and his older sister Rachel all the way from where they lived in Chicago and left them with their grandparents while the parents took a trip to Montreal and Quebec City.

Daniel got confused during the night, woke to go the bathroom, and forgot where he was. He went in the wrong direction and fell down the stairs. His left arm was broken and his head was bruised, but otherwise he was all right, except for the terror of tumbling down an entire flight of stairs and the fear he was left with of strange, unfamiliar places. Anxiety and sleeplessness when he first moved to New York were what brought him to see Gwen in the first place.

Carly has noticed that Gwen writes about Daniel in a much more personal tone than when she writes about her other patients. Lots of times she adds poetic descriptions of how the sky looks or how the sunlight slants across the room and makes his hair look more golden. She has a theory that Gwen's actually in love with Daniel, even though Carly knows psychiatrists aren't supposed to do that with their patients.

At 110th Street the bus turns west and begins to cross town. The north end of Central Park lays out on the left, just south of Harlem, the dangerous part of the park Carly is never supposed to go into by herself. As she passes Lasker Pool, which has been cleared of ice and is waiting for summer to become a swimming pool instead of a skating rink, Carly thinks that maybe sometime when she has nothing better to do, she'll take a walk around up here and see what it's like.

The mother and daughter with the pink barrettes get off at Broadway, two stops before the bus turns north onto Riverside Drive. Only a few people are left on the bus now, some college student types and an old Black man who keeps cutting his eyes at Beacon, as though he's expecting the dog to make a threatening move.

At ll6th Street and Riverside, Daniel and Beacon get off, and Carly gets off behind them. She pauses to cup her hands and light up a cigarette before following them up the hill to Broadway, through the main gates, and across the Columbia campus. When they reach an archway outside the bookstore, Daniel digs into his pocket for a slip of paper and tacks it to a board with lots of other notices. Carly takes note that it's a green piece of paper and continues following him across campus.

Carly has never been to Columbia before, and she's amazed at the existence within New York City of such a great and formal courtyard, of the perfectly straight hedgerows that line the well-ordered maze of pathways that lead to imposing buildings with oxidized green copper roofs that form the enclosure that separates this other world, almost like a magical kingdom in a storybook, from the messy, dirty streets outside.

When they exit the gates at the other side of campus, Daniel turns north on Amsterdam Avenue. At 119th Street, he makes a right turn and goes to the end of the block to a building with *Butler Hall* carved in the stone over the doorway. Carly recognizes from references in Gwen's notebook that this is where Daniel lives. Most Columbia students live in the dorms, but because of Daniel's special situation, living in a residential apartment building has been a better arrangement for him and Beacon.

Instead of heading inside, Daniel and Beacon walk back a few paces in her direction, where Carly leans up against a tree. As Daniel approaches, she feels herself go prickly with panic, but then she remembers that not only does Daniel not know who she is, he couldn't see her standing here dragging nervously on a cigarette, watching his every move, even if he did.

Just before reaching the spot where Carly is standing, Daniel lets go of Beacon's harness. The dog sniffs around, lifts a leg, and pees on a car tire. After a few more sniffs, the dog squats in the gutter, and Carly sees his tail twitch as he takes a dump.

Daniel is standing no more than four feet away from Carly. Now that she sees him at such close range, he looks even hand-somer than she realized. His clear skin has an outdoorsy glow, and she takes in how tall and muscular he is. Standing safely invisible, barely breathing, Carly looks him up and down. She examines his broad shoulders, his narrow hips, the firm, rounded thigh muscles that press gently against the fabric of his jeans. She notices his strong forearms, which hang bare below the rolled sleeves of his light blue shirt, and imagines him lifting weights.

Carly wonders if he goes out with girls and what it would be like to do stuff with him. She knows Gwen's patients lie on the couch when they talk to her, and even though Carly thinks it's ridiculous and far-fetched, she can't help wondering if Gwen ever has horny thoughts like the ones Carly's having right now.

Suddenly, she's overcome by shame. She feels like a voy-eur or a Peeping Tom, staring at this man who has no way of knowing he's being watched. She suddenly wants to leave, to pull away and make silent amends for taking advantage of a dis-advantaged person, but she doesn't dare move.

As soon as the dog finishes squatting and twitching his tail, he trots right over to Daniel, who takes up the harness and walks back to the entrance of Butler Hall. Carly hears herself let out her long-held breath.

Daniel and Beacon disappear inside, and Carly walks back toward Broadway. When she gets to the bookstore, she stops and checks the note Daniel posted on the board. *Reader wanted for blind student. $6/hr. Flexible hours.* She digs around for a pen and paper but realizes she doesn't have any. Impulsively, she tears Daniel's message off the board and tucks it in her pocket.

Checking her Swatch, she sees that it's after six o'clock. Overhead is almost dark, a deep purple shot with fading light. You could make a tie-dyed T-shirt, Carly thinks, with the turquoise and fuchsia that streak across the sky.

CHAPTER THREE

When Carly lets herself into the apartment, this time through the front door, she hears running water and clonking pots and realizes her mother's rushing around to fix the dinner that Carly should have remembered to put up. Her mother's first evening session begins at seven thirty, so there's not much time to get food cooked and eaten and cleared away if nothing's ready ahead of time.

"Hi there," Carly hears her mother call out, "where've you been?" It's not exactly anger that she detects in her mother's voice. It's that other something, the tone of silent warfare that gets layered over the anger to disguise it so Carly will think her mother doesn't mind that she never does anything she's asked to do. The one who shows the least emotion wins the war. Carly learned this long ago, the hard way, by losing control of herself. It has happened over and over again.

"I forgot a book and had to go back to school to get it," Carly calls out, and then rushes upstairs to her bedroom so her mother won't catch her empty-handed.

The unmade bed and piles of clothes strewn all about feel familiar and comforting as Carly enters her room and shuts the door tight behind her. She pulls the black wool sweater over her head and tosses it across the room, where it falls on a magazine with Mick Jagger's face on the cover. Throwing herself on her bed, she dangles an arm down over the side of the mattress and feels around under the tangle of blankets and sheets that have spilled onto the floor until she finds a worn gray flannel squirrel, which she stuffs into the crook of her arm. "Squirrelkin" is the nickname her father has always called her. Now that she's older, even though it's still comforting, Carly sometimes feels self-conscious cuddling a stuffed animal.

It's scary, and very powerful, to think about what she has just done. If her mother knew where she really had been, what would she say? A thought flickers across Carly's mind, and even though it's too wild for her to believe this could happen, Carly imagines talking to Daniel as though they were close friends and his telling her about the therapist he goes to see.

The issue of appearance doesn't come up, of course, because Daniel can't see that Gwen's tall and slim with short, straight blonde hair tucked behind her ears or pulled back in a clump with a thick tortoiseshell barrette. Daniel can't think in terms of whether Gwen looks better in skirts or slacks or wearing clingy sweaters or silk blouses rolled casually at the cuff with a couple buttons open at the top the way she does. But Carly wonders how he feels with Gwen and how they get along. She tries to imagine what Gwen sounds like talking to Daniel, which of her many tones of voice she uses to draw him out and make him feel at ease talking about himself and telling his most personal secrets.

It's hard for Carly, who's so closed and reserved, to imagine what her mother could do to make a person open up to her. Does she have a special voice, different from any Carly has heard, which she saves just for patients and packs away, like the notebooks, when the patients leave? And is the voice the same for each one, or does she invent a new one, like an actor creating a new character role?

"She's really very nice and very sympathetic," Carly imagines Daniel telling her, over coffee in some student café somewhere near Columbia. "I can talk to her about anything, and she always understands."

Carly knows from reading the notes that Daniel misses Gwen when he's away from her, thinks about her longingly, even has dreams about her that he relates in the sessions. Was he sad, Carly wonders, when he left this afternoon? She thinks back and remembers the quiet, calm expression on his face as he stood waiting for the bus, before the little girl came up and asked about the dog. And yes, come to think of it, he did look a little sad.

With a knock on Carly's door, Gwen announces that dinner's ready. Carly's suddenly aware of being exhausted and can't find the energy to rouse herself from the bed. Her arms and legs feel leaden and won't propel themselves into action. She's still lying on her stomach, and now she tries to force herself into motion. Carly concentrates very hard, visualizing the little cells called neurons moving around and sending messages. She can actually feel a buzzing in her brain, like a key turning in a car ignition, but the motor won't turn over.

With a tremendous surge of will, Carly kicks one leg over the side of the bed and lurches to her feet. A dizzy feeling makes the room feel like it's spinning slowly around her, and she waits before attempting a first step toward the door.

The image of the yellow grizzle on the raw chicken nauseates her, and she remembers that she has had nothing but a few Oreos to eat all day. She'd like to tell her mother that she's tired or that she isn't feeling well, but she knows that Gwen has gone back downstairs to put dinner on and that she wouldn't be particularly sympathetic if she heard Carly's excuses.

The butcher-block table in the kitchen is laid out with three place settings, one at either end and one in the middle, facing out from the wall. A ceramic bowl filled with chartreuse apples that look waxed they're so perfectly smooth. Three knives to the right of each place and three forks to the left set on three paper napkins folded corner to corner in points that remind Carly of the way she used to draw a boat when she was little: an upside-down triangle with a line up the center for the mast, and then two more triangles for the sails. Salad plates bordered with blue and yellow bands to the left and an empty glass to the right of three matching dinner plates. It would make a perfect setting, Carly thinks, for one of her father's ads: a mother making dinner for a daughter who feels sick and exhausted but gets her appetite back when the magical meal is served.

His latest ad shows a yuppie couple getting ready for work. They sit side by side over clear glass coffee cups, and the wife's coffee is darker and, supposedly (since you can't smell TV ads), more aromatic than the husband's. He gets jealous, tastes hers, and announces he's a convert to the stronger, better brand. The wife gives him a perky little kiss, and in a know-it-all voice that Carly finds annoying, she tells him that now he can make the best blend for both of them. You just know she's got the upper hand in everything, kind of like Carly's mom.

"Where's Dad?" Carly asks.

Gwen is pouring water. "Late, as usual. And by the way, Ms. Harrington called to set up a meeting in her office tomorrow after school. She wants you and me both to be there, Carly."

"I'm surprised Ms. Harrington even knows who I am," Carly says as her dad comes through the front door and calls out, "I'm home, everyone."

"Dinner's on," Gwen calls from the kitchen as Joel shucks off his jacket on the chair in the foyer, the way he always does.

He comes into the kitchen with that hangdog look Carly knows he gets when he's feeling guilty. She hates this scenario, which plays itself out more and more, over and over again.

Carly knows her dad's trying to sound chipper as he says, "Hey, Squirrelkin, what's up? How was your day?"

"You're already in deep shit for being late," Carly tells him as he hugs her hello.

"Yeah, well, there's this thing called work, you know . . ." Her dad's saying this more for her mom, Carly knows, than for her.

"Food's getting cold," Gwen calls. The image of the couple drinking coffee in Joel's ad pops into Carly's mind, and she wishes her dad would just say something nice and go up to her mom and give her a hug.

Instead, he sits down at his place at the table, unfolds the paper napkin, and tucks it in the space between his neck and the second button of his shirt. Carly knows he does this when he has something to do after dinner and doesn't want to get his shirt dirty, but she hates the way it makes her father look, like a little kid with a bib around his neck.

"Going back to the office after dinner?" Carly asks him.

"We're putting to bed the campaign for Victoria's Secret."

"Are there discounts on bras and panties in it for me?" Carly asks.

"Their ads of women in scanty underwear are so tasteless and retro," Gwen says as she hands Joel and Carly their plates with chicken, carrot pennies, and a pile of white rice.

Carly catches Joel's look of dejection out of the corner of her eye. She wishes he'd retaliate, shoot back with a clever reply, but he just sits there looking like an animal that got struck. Gwen's back is turned as she serves out a portion for herself.

To change the subject, and even though it's not true but

as a kind of test, Carly announces, "By the way, Lauren's mom invited me to dinner on Sunday."

Gwen whirls around from the stove. "But that's your birthday, Carly. You never told me."

"And when exactly between being at the hospital and seeing patients all day and night was there a chance to tell you?"

"Carly! Don't be rude to your mother."

With her back still turned to the stove, Gwen asks, "You don't think it's rude being late all the time for dinner?"

Joel ignores the question and applies himself to cutting up his chicken.

Gwen sits down with her plate and shifts into a softer tone of voice. "I thought the three of us would go to dinner and the movies for your birthday the way we always do."

"Well, no one said anything about it, so I made other plans."

"I really feel badly about this," Joel says, rousing himself from his chicken cutting. "But it winds up we have an ad campaign in California, and I'll have to leave on the weekend to be there on time for Monday's meeting."

Carly's heart sinks when she realizes that both her parents have completely blown off her birthday, but she wants to keep it light, so she tells her dad, "It's no big deal. If you have to work, you have to work."

"It *is* a big deal, a sixteenth birthday," Gwen says, "and I was hoping we could do something special to celebrate together."

"Which is why we were just gonna do dinner and a movie like we do every other year?"

Gwen looks caught off guard but comes back with, "We could still make plans for Saturday to do something special together, the three of us."

Joel's face is getting red the way it does when he gets flustered. "But I'm leaving on Saturday."

Carly sees her mom react with surprise. "Like it takes forty-eight hours to fly to California," Gwen sneers.

"Look, I feel awful about this, but Edwin didn't realize it was Carly's birthday. He went and scheduled the shooting for next week, and it can't be changed now."

"And why on earth would your swooshy assistant have a clue about when my birthday is?"

Carly has never liked Edwin. Whenever she calls her dad and Edwin answers, he acts as if he doesn't recognize her, even though they've met when Carly has gone to Joel's office on the way to a movie or dinner after work. "Mr. Klein's in a meeting," Edwin always tells her in his obnoxious, nasal voice. "May I know who's calling?" "No message," Carly always says, and hangs up. She's not about to stoop to his level.

Joel abruptly stands up and carries his plate over to the stove. "Seconds, anyone?" Even though it's almost as full as when Gwen handed it to him, he adds a scoop of carrots and holds out the pot with the serving spoon toward the table.

"For goodness' sake, Joel, just sit down so we can eat."

Joel notices that Carly hasn't touched her dinner. He gazes into her face with squinty eyes, the way he looks when he's concentrating on something difficult to figure out. "You look thinner, Squirrelkin. Have you been eating right?"

"For Chrissake, Dad. I'm almost sixteen years old, and my name's Carly!"

"Joel!" Gwen glares at him with a don't-go-there look meant to warn him off the topic of Carly's weight.

Carly starts moving carrots from one side of her plate to the other. To change the subject, she asks her father about the California ad campaign. "So what's the new shoot about?"

"OP hired us to showcase their summer swimwear. We're shooting in Malibu."

"Oh, so now we're doing teenagers in bikinis?"

"Give it a break, Mom."

Carly expects her father to look hurt and go silent, but instead he laughs and blurts out, "If feminists had their way, I suppose girls would go swimming in jackets and ties."

"Don't be ridiculous, Joel."

Carly can't be sure, but she detects an undercurrent in her parents' comments. Her mom doesn't sound exactly jealous, but between the attack on Victoria's Secret models and bikini-wearing teenagers and Joel's dig about feminists, some message is being sent.

Even though they've barely touched their dinners, Gwen looks at her watch and announces that it's time for her to get ready for her evening session. She picks up her plate and, like an afterthought, asks Carly, "By the way, what happened with starting dinner?"

"I didn't know I was supposed to," Carly says.

"Didn't you see the note on the fridge?"

"I didn't go into the kitchen," Carly lies, but the moment she does she sees her book bag on the floor by the back door, where she left it a few hours ago.

"What are your books still doing on the floor over there, then?"

Carly can't miss the singsong sound of victory in her mother's voice. "And why can't you cook dinner the way everyone else's mom does?"

"For the same reason half-naked women in Victoria's Secret ads are stereotypes that set women back half a century!"

Gwen hasn't raised her voice, but it's obvious she's furious now. Carly grabs her plate, stands up, and shouts as loud as she can, "Well, I'm not your maid, and you're not my boss. Would you fucking please get off my case?" Tossing her plate filled with food in the sink, she runs out of the kitchen and upstairs to her room.

CHAPTER FOUR

arly doodles animal lairs and tree houses, cave dwellings and log cabins, while Ms. Cribben is handing back last week's essay. She starts at the front right corner of the room with Harper Phyffe's paper and frames her closed-mouth smile that makes her eyes wrinkle at the corners as she places it carefully in front of her.

"Good job, Harper," Ms. Cribben says, and everyone in the class automatically translates, "Straight A."

Carly's English teacher is a huge lady with a net covering her thinning gray curls and lingerie straps that are constantly falling down off her shoulders underneath her gauzy, see-through blouses. Every few moments in the middle of teaching, Ms. Cribben plunges her pudgy pink hand into her blouse and rescues a dangling strap. Carly's so apprehensive that this will happen and so distracted when it does that she can barely concentrate on what Ms. Cribben's saying.

The class is doing a unit on medieval literature for which Ms. Cribben makes them memorize long lists of Old English words and gives them weekly quizzes on terms like *halberd* and *fiefdom* and *droit du seigneur*. Spelling counts as much as meaning.

By the time Ms. Cribben works her way around to Carly, who sits toward the back on the left, she has given out half a dozen "good job's," three "very nice's," and "a lot of progress here" to Jodie Killingsworth. All the rest of the papers were returned with no comment—translation: B/B- range.

When Ms. Cribben drops Carly's essay on her desk, it makes a louder plop than the others. Did she hold it higher, Carly wonders, or did she drop it harder, to make its landing on Carly's desk loud enough so heads turn? A very large red *D* is slanted conspicuously across the title page, larger, Carly thinks, than the size of the other grades on the papers all around her. As she walks on to the next row, Ms. Cribben turns her head back toward Carly and says, very loud, "Ms. Harrington expects you in her office directly after class, Carly. Without the gum in your mouth. I don't suppose there's anything you can do now about the color of your blouse."

The room is silent until laughter breaks out all around as everyone takes note of the fact that Carly's blouse is pale yellow instead of regulation white. Carly glances at the comments on her essay, makes an "it figures" face, stuffs the paper in her book bag, and collects herself to leave. When the school bell rings and Carly stands, one navy knee sock sinks down around her ankle.

Heading out of the classroom, Harper Phyffe goes out of her way to pass Carly's desk. She makes a conspicuous display of adjusting the pink-and-blue polka-dotted scarf she's wearing around her neck as she taunts, "You have to get good grades if you wanna tweak the dress code."

As Carly makes her way down the hall toward Ms. Harrington's office, a band of senior girls is coming from the opposite direction wearing very short plaid gym shorts, color-coordinated tops, and athletic socks. They sling hockey sticks over their shoulders and strut through the halls like an army squadron heading for battle.

Harper pushes past Carly and catches up with them, and even though she's just a sophomore, she links arms with Joan Ellen Barnwell, the captain of the team. "See you at Saturday's game, Harper," Joan Ellen coos. "We're counting on you!" Carly can't help resenting the fact that Harper's not only the smartest girl in the class, she's also the best athlete.

Carly opens a heavy wood door and enters the hushed atmosphere of the carpeted reception area. She stops before a secretary's desk, where a woman in a crisp gray suit with large tortoiseshell eyeglasses is picking up a ringing telephone.

"Baxter School, Office of the Headmistress. How may I help you?"

The secretary pauses to listen.

"Very good, Mrs. Davenport. I'll ring you right through."

She buzzes an intercom and announces in a clipped, no-nonsense voice, "Mrs. Penelope Davenport on line three, Ms. Harrington."

She hangs up the phone and looks up at Carly. "Yes?" Her voice is charmless and impatient, as though she's being disturbed.

"Ms. Harrington wants to see me," Carly says.

"Your name and class?"

"Carly Klein. Sophomore."

The secretary indicates a bench against the wall and tells Carly, "Take a seat."

She goes over to a large filing cabinet on the back wall and removes a folder. Armed, she walks across the reception area to a paneled door with Willoughby Harrington's name on a brass plate, makes a little rhythmic knock on the door, and enters.

Carly sits on the bench and crosses her arms. She's chewing her gum in an absent-minded way, then suddenly remembers and swallows hard. Carly knows she's not stupid, but her mom's background has been a hard act to follow. Gwen went to Smith, a women's college that she credits with liberating her from her father's and older brothers' domination. That's why she chose Baxter before Carly was old enough to choose for herself. Because she was such a fast learner—she read the captions to *New Yorker* cartoons when she was four—Carly skipped pre-K and went straight to kindergarten.

She did very well in the early years, but physically she has been a slow developer. She didn't start growing breasts till thirteen and didn't get her period till fourteen. Lately, her grades have been dropping along with her interest in her studies. She can't concentrate in class, and doing homework assignments is getting harder and harder.

Her favorite book, when she was younger, was *Little House on the Prairie*. In spite of being fifteen going on sixteen, she regularly watches episodes on TV, and she rereads it occasionally. If Carly could choose, she'd live a century ago, before electricity and automobiles and all the elaborate "conveniences" of modern life. She'd wear long skirts and heavy boots and grow her own food. Her husband would hunt and forage, and they'd cook wild game and fresh fish for supper every night. They'd have half a dozen kids at least, and the boys would hunt with their father and the girls would stay home and cook and sew with Carly.

She knows she's out of step with her own time. Harper and her clique are busy collecting bright-colored clothing from the Gap and planning careers as neurosurgeons and senators. Baxter's headmistress wears vests and ties and gives pep talks at Monday morning assembly about how girls can do anything. Carly knows that by "anything," Ms. Harrington doesn't mean cooking meals and making babies.

The secretary comes out and tells her, "You may go in now."

Willoughby Harrington's office is very large. The dark walnut bookcases are neatly arranged with books and journals. A crystal vase with yellow daffodils accents her large oval desk amidst squarely stacked piles of papers. Ms. Harrington, whose silver-gray hair is pulled tightly back in a bun, is in the process of signing documents with a ballpoint pen. Carly figures the inkwell with a feather quill that's prominently displayed at the center of her desk, right in front of the chair that Ms. Harrington waves Carly into, is just for show.

"Your mother called a little while ago to say she couldn't make our meeting today. Something about a hospital emergency. I would have thought your declining school performance would constitute a competing emergency." Ms. Harrington pauses, and when Carly doesn't say anything, she adds, "Apparently not."

Carly squirms uncomfortably, not sure if she's supposed to defend herself or her mother.

"I understand that your work has been suffering lately, Carly. Ms. Cribben tells me that your English grade has dropped from a B average to a D."

She raises an eyebrow, eyes Carly intently, and waits for a response.

"Ms. Cribben disagrees with my interpretation of Chaucer's 'Wife of Bath's Tale,'" Carly tells her.

"And Mr. Hess reports that you're in danger of failing chemistry."

Carly is studying the pattern of the Oriental rug as Ms. Harrington speaks.

"A notice has been sent home, and I've requested a conference with your parents, at which you shall be present, to review these matters."

Carly feels the first drumbeats of apprehension. Ms. Harrington raises her eyebrow again, the same one, and tells Carly,

"Well, we hope you can pull yourself together and bring your academic performance up to standard." She scrutinizes Carly and continues, "Unless something else is going on that we don't know about?"

Carly senses that the interview is ending. She gets to her feet and says, "Right. I mean, no, everything's fine. I mean, sure. I can do better."

Ms. Harrington rises too.

"Good, Carly, we'll count on that. Baxter's a place for the most highly motivated, hardest-working girls. A lot of very capable students would like to come to us, but we only have space for the best."

Carly senses the threat but does not respond.

"And one more thing, Carly. We do have a uniform dress code here at Baxter, and unlike literature, it is not a matter of individual interpretation."

CHAPTER
FIVE

When Carly rings the Lenskys' doorbell after school, Lauren opens the door looking annoyed. "How come you're late?"

"I had to intercept a letter to my parents from the headmistress at Baxter before my mom goes through the mail."

"Trouble at the Princess Palace?"

Carly's never quite sure how she feels about Lauren's negative comments about Baxter. On the one hand, Carly agrees with most of them, but it rankles her that Lauren is so judgmental about a situation over which Carly has no control.

"I was called into the office today. Bad grades and stuff, the usual. A notice was sent home. Oh, and my mom was supposed to be at the meeting with the headmistress, but she blew it off."

"Sounds serious. If you're lucky, they'll kick you out and you can transfer to Newton."

"Fat chance! Anyway, with what my parents pay to send me to Baxter, they can't kick me out."

"Don't be so sure. A girl in my class got kicked out of Chapin, and her father's a gazillionaire who owns diamond mines. Hey, I have to get something altered at the tailor's. Wanna come?"

Even though they go to different schools, Lauren and Carly are best friends and take classes together at the Art Students League of New York on the weekends. At Newton, the very liberal coed school in Greenwich Village where Lauren goes, the kids call the teachers by their first names, and if you're not in the mood to learn something, you can substitute learning something else. Lauren substitutes art for math, science, and gym. Newton doesn't have uniforms, so Lauren can wear anything she wants, including jeans. Mostly she wears black tights, big black sweaters that hang low around her hips, and black leather shoes with heavy soles and shiny silver sprockets. She wears eyeliner and mascara to school, too, and even very bright red lipstick.

The Kleins live in apartment 11-12A, a duplex in the front of the building, and even though they have two floors, more rooms, and a view of the park, Carly likes Lauren's apartment much better than her own. For one, the Lenskys' place is always a mess, while the Kleins' is so neat and clean you can't possibly feel at home. Lauren says it feels like being in a museum with ropes around the furniture displays so you'll know you're not supposed to sit.

The other big difference is Lauren's mother, who's French and the only mother Carly knows who insists that you call her by her first name, Tibou. If you happen to call her Mrs. Lensky, she rakes her hands through her flyaway, reddish-gray hair and, even though Carly's much younger, exclaims, "*Mais non, ma vieille, il faut m'appeler Tibou!*" The first time Tibou said this, Lauren translated: "No, old friend, you must call me Tibou." When she greets you, she kisses both cheeks.

About her name, Tibou explains that when she was born she was very tiny and premature, so her mother called her "*petit bout*," which means "little bit." The name was used so much by everyone that it got shortened and stuck. The amazing thing is, Lauren's mother is five feet, ten and a half inches tall.

Carly's tall for her age and already bigger than Gwen. It feels good standing near Tibou, like being sheltered beneath the bower of a tree. Carly likes to imagine being Tibou's other daughter. Lauren would be her sister instead of her best friend, and Carly wouldn't be an only child anymore. She would get to live full-time in the Lensky home instead of just once in a while sleeping over.

When Carly and Lauren come into the kitchen, Tibou is wrapped in a red-and-yellow-checkered apron, and her flyaway hair is tied back in a scarf. Lauren's younger brother, Marc, who's eight, sits at the counter sculpting pie dough into a large round object with ears.

"*Mon Dieu, de petits fascistes!*" Tibou cries out as she sees Carly in her regulation plaid uniform. Lauren explains, "Tibou thinks that wearing school uniforms is fundamentally undemocratic."

The Lenskys are very political minded and talk all the time about the fall of communism and the desirability of a nuclear freeze. When countries are invaded or hostage crises occur, the whole family stays up until midnight and watches news bulletins on the big, blocky television that takes up practically an entire wall of their living room. Tibou even let Lauren stay home from school the morning after watching late-night reports of Tiananmen Square.

"My mother thinks school uniforms cut down on competition," Carly tells them, "but the girls at Baxter are the most competitive kids I've ever met."

"*Quelle hypocrisie*," Tibou comments as she whisks a bowl full of egg whites.

"We're having ginger soufflé for dessert. I separated the eggs," Marc declares.

"Wow. I'm impressed," Lauren says. "A prepubescent James Beard."

"I set the table," Marc announces. "You have to clean up, Lauren."

"I don't take orders from punks," she says.

The Lenskys' apartment always smells of delicious foods. Tibou cooks "nouvelle cuisine," and the simplest meal is like a dish in a fancy restaurant. They have the same kitchen as the Kleins', laid out in the opposite direction, but instead of being wallpapered with flowers, theirs is painted high-gloss white with ceiling-high pegboards designed by Mr. Lensky. Dozens of different tools and implements hang from little metal hooks that stick out from the holes: garlic presses and wire whips in several sizes and a cheese grater that turns in your hand like a can opener.

Dented copper pots and pans in every shape and size dangle from a hanging pot rack, and on the counter near the stove a wire basket holds a few dozen eggs. A rope of real garlic hangs from the wall, and fresh herbs grow in little clay pots on the windowsill. Tibou snips them with scissors and sprinkles them over the food she cooks. In the Kleins' kitchen, everything is kept in drawers and cabinets or in the refrigerator.

When Marc sticks his tongue out at Lauren, she flips him a finger and drags Carly off by the arm. "We're heading out," she calls behind her, flipping a black wool skirt—a mere scrap of fabric—over her shoulder. "Carly's coming with me to get this altered."

"Papa will be home in an hour, Lauren," Tibou calls out. "Dinner at six thirty."

As they set off toward Madison Avenue, Lauren sticks a cigarette in her mouth and asks Carly if she has a light.

"Must be nice to need a wardrobe," Carly says, flicking a Bic lighter for Lauren. "Drag?"

Lauren passes the cigarette and looks Carly over in her plaid school uniform. "I don't know how you stand wearing that thing every day."

"It's not like I have a choice," Carly says as she retrieves Ms. Harrington's letter from her pocket, tears it in two, and drops it in a garbage pail on the corner of Ninety-Sixth and Madison.

Mr. Laszlo runs a little narrow shop between Sal the shoemaker's and Mr. Marx's jewelry store. His window is filled with plants, some that grow up from below, some that hang down from above. Long, leafy vines hide the inside of his tiny shop from the street so you can change behind his folding screen when you have your clothes altered.

Cats lounge all over Mr. Laszlo's shop, more than Carly can keep track of. She tries to count them, but they move around, change places, and look alike. Big tigers and tabbies that lick their paws and settle contentedly on the counter, on top of the heavy metal wardrobe, at Mr. Laszlo's feet as he pumps the pedal of his large black sewing machine.

While Lauren disappears behind the screen to change, Mr. Laszlo goes over to the wardrobe, opens the lock, and pulls out a shoebox of photographs he has taken.

"Here," he says, plunking down the box in Carly's lap. "To keep busy the hands while you wait."

He speaks with a heavy Hungarian accent and squints as he smiles behind extra thick lenses that he pulls down onto the tip of his nose.

Mr. Laszlo's work has been shown and written about in newspapers and magazines. She shuffles through stacks and stacks of photographs—all black-and-white, all sad, sickly faces and seedy scenes of New York City life and homeless people huddled in doorways with shopping carts loaded with blankets and tattered clothing. Drug-addled teenagers sit listlessly on the stoops of Harlem tenements. A half-naked child runs barefoot in the gutter with a mother no older than Carly standing by helplessly, her pregnant belly protruding like a ship's prow. Carly knows that art need not be pretty to be beautiful, but she thinks this is maybe going too far.

"I want this shorter," Lauren says as she emerges from behind the screen.

Mr. Laszlo registers astonishment. "You sure you don't want longer?" he asks, and Lauren shakes her head.

She catches Carly's eye, and they suppress their laughter as Mr. Laszlo slowly trundles across the shop. While Lauren turns slowly in a circle towering above him, Mr. Laszlo squats at her heels and uses a tiny press like a bicycle pump to puff out a line of white powder dashes all around the hem of her skirt.

"Shorter," Lauren tells him impatiently. "To here," she says, pointing at the middle of her thigh.

"You are sure? So short you want?"

Mr. Laszlo squints and smiles up at her, and Lauren says flatly, "I'm sure."

He adjusts his measuring press and puffs another line of white powder dashes just above the first line. When he's through, Lauren stands back and examines herself in the thin strip of mirror on the wall beside the folding screen. She spreads her hands wide and pats her behind, smoothing the fabric over her hips and buttocks.

"Can you make it a little tighter across here?" she asks, indicating a place just below her crotch.

Mr. Laszlo's voice cracks as he asks, "Tighter?"

"Um-hum," Lauren tells him, and spins around to see the rear view over her shoulder.

Mr. Laszlo sets his mouth in an unnaturally wide smile and lines his teeth with straight pins. They stick out like spokes from a wheel, forming a perfect semicircle.

"Hands by sides now, very still," he coaxes Lauren, and with the speed of lightning, he pokes the straight pins, one after another—flashes of silver—into invisible tucks and creases of Lauren's skirt.

"Tighter," Lauren tells him, sucking in her breath and making her tummy concave.

Mr. Laszlo nods, his teeth still clenched around the few remaining pins.

"Tighter."

He talks like a ventriloquist, his mouth barely moving as he forms the word. "Tighter. Yes?"

He's nodding his head vigorously to show that he gets it. The silver straight pins glint in the light that filters through the plant-filled window.

As Lauren changes behind the screen, Mr. Laszlo tells a story. He pumps the pedal of his machine and speaks into the air, not to anyone in particular. His squinty eyes open wide, spittle gathers in the corners of his mouth, and his breath comes fast as he describes how he had to pass a test in "the old country" before becoming a tailor. He tells how carefully he had to sew, making no mistakes at all, so none of the white thread he was required to use would show against the black fabric of the suit he was sewing. When Mr. Laszlo finishes his story, he sighs heavily as though just the remembering and telling have tired him out.

"How could you do that?" Carly asks him, and he tells her:

"I wanted to be a tailor, so I did it."

Lauren emerges from behind the screen and tosses the skirt on the counter.

"What do you say we use black thread on this one?" she says. "When do you think I can get this back?"

"When you need for?" Mr. Laszlo asks.

"As soon as possible."

"You come back in a few days. I have ready for you when you come back."

As they leave the shop, Carly wonders what the message is in the story Mr. Laszlo told. She thinks of the depressing photographs, then of Lauren's very short, very tight skirt, and she gets the idea that Mr. Laszlo is judging them, lumping everything here in the "new country" together: the short, tight skirts, the unwed mothers, the hungry, dirty, needy children. Lauren takes out another cigarette and asks Carly for a light.

When they reach their building, Lauren drops her cigarette on the sidewalk and grinds it out. As they wait in the lobby for the elevator, Carly mentions casually to Lauren that when school's over, she's going to summer camp.

"How long's your sentence?" Lauren asks. "And where's this internment camp located?"

"It's some ranch in Colorado that my mother found to park me for the summer."

"Why don't you just come to Vermont and stay with us?"

"I wish I could, but my mother has this thing about 'structured' time and activity."

"Then at least come for dinner on Sunday," Lauren says.

"Sunday's my birthday."

"So what do you have planned?"

"Not much," Carly says. "My parents kind of forgot. And my dad's going out of town for work."

"Then it's settled."

"What about your mom? Don't you have to ask?"

"Tibou's not the issue here." Lauren calls her mother by her first name. "Do you wanna come or not?"

"Of course I'll come," Carly says fast, trying to sound as sure of herself as Lauren. She feels relieved to have an actual invitation from the Lenskys.

As the elevator opens, a tall, thin woman wearing a trench coat and carrying a briefcase emerges. Carly recognizes her as Doris, the patient whose husband died in a car crash last year. She looks Carly and Lauren up and down and walks on.

"What's her problem?" Lauren asks. "You know her or something?"

"She's one of my mother's mental cases."

Lauren rolls her eyes. "She obviously needs work."

"Did you ever see the blind guy with the seeing-eye dog?" Carly asks. "I followed him when he left the other day. He's a junior at Columbia."

"Did you meet him, or what?" Lauren wants to know.

"No, I didn't meet him. I just followed him to see where he lives."

"What a waste. You should've made a move." Lauren shakes her head disapprovingly and then adds, "How do you know he's a junior?"

"My mother's notes. She leaves them around after her sessions. Not only that, I saw him put this notice up with his phone number to get readers. I might call him sometime."

"You should call him before you leave for camp. He might change his number."

CHAPTER SIX

Gwen opens Carly's door and calls in from the hall, "Anything you need before I leave for my meeting?"

"Thanks for knocking before opening my door."

"Do you have a lot of homework left?" Gwen asks.

Carly kicks away from her desk and swirls around on her swivel chair. "Give it a break, Mom. You already asked about my homework at dinner."

"You'll chip the paint if you keep doing that with your feet on the desk, Carly."

"I don't give a damn about this ugly old desk."

"It so happens to have also been my desk when I was a girl, and I'd like to see it survive for a few more years."

"You should give it to a museum then."

"I'll be back by ten. Try to get your work done early enough to get a good night's sleep. Exams are coming up, and it's important to be well rested."

The moment she hears the front door close, Carly strips off her uniform and pulls on a pair of her tightest jeans and a black turtleneck sweater that comes practically to her knees. Grabbing a pair of black flats and her parka from the floor where she dropped it several hours ago, Carly races to the door and checks through the peephole to see that Gwen isn't standing in the hall. Instead of the elevator, Carly takes the stairs two at a time and emerges through the service entrance to her apartment building so the doorman on duty won't see her leaving.

Once out on the street, Carly takes off in a sprint toward Madison Avenue. She sees a taxi with its rooftop sign lit up, sticks two index fingers in her mouth, and lets out a loud whistle. The cab squeals to a stop right beside her. She knows from the notes in Gwen's notebook that Daniel's playing saxophone tonight at the Downunder Café on the Columbia campus.

When Carly gets out on Broadway, the January sky is cracked with clouds brightened by an invisible moon. She walks briskly, trying to look as though she's often out on nights like this. She has heard stories of rapes that have taken place around the city. People are always saying how important it is to look like you know where you're going and to be purposeful about getting there.

A random thought floats through her mind, the image of herself being pounced upon by some unknown man. She has already made up her mind, long ago when she first learned that men sometimes take women by force, that she wouldn't fight back or resist in any way. If it happened when she was trailing Daniel, Carly wonders if the dog would turn on his heels and come to her rescue.

The Downunder Café has high ceilings with exposed pipes and cinder-block walls. It looks more like an alleyway than a room. Clumps of college students are huddled around, talking in low voices and drinking from Styrofoam cups. A girl with dark eye makeup and lustrous hennaed hair flipped all to one side comes by with a big jug in one hand and a stack of cups in the other.

"Want some?" she asks Carly.

"Yeah, thanks," Carly says, trying to sound self-confident.

The girl pours too much, and red wine overflows the cup and runs onto Carly's jeans. She jumps back a step and blurts out, "Sorry," even though she realizes as she does that she shouldn't be the one to apologize.

"That'll be a dollar fifty," the girl tells Carly, who hadn't realized the wine was for sale. She fumbles in her jeans pockets and comes up with a handful of change, which she counts out laboriously and hands to the girl, who has been shifting her weight impatiently from one foot to the other while waiting.

Some of the students are sitting on the shabby sofas that line the room behind the tables and chairs that fill the rest of the space. Wine bottles drizzled with candle wax rise like ruined sandcastles in the center of each table. Besides a track of dimmed lights that runs overhead, the flames from the bottles are the sole source of light. They flicker and cast wobbly shadows on the walls.

Daniel stands by himself, saxophone in hand and Beacon by his side, in the far corner, as though waiting for something before what's going to happen can happen. The dog sits patiently, his chin arched upward toward his master like a seal sticking its head up for air. From across the room they appear in black silhouette. Carly thinks they look very statuesque. She decides that if she were to sculpt them, she'd carve them out of a single lump of clay.

Someone in the middle of the room snaps on a floodlight that illuminates the center stage area. The light that it casts makes Daniel and Beacon look alive, like wax figures in a museum that suddenly take on the aspect and animation of real living beings. Someone else is adjusting a floor mike, repeating the words, "Testing, one, two, three," over and over at varying volumes. Carly is only vaguely aware of the commotion around her as people start shuffling chairs and settling down at tables.

A guy with long hair pulled back in a ponytail goes over to Daniel and places a hand on his arm. Carly can see them exchanging words, and then Daniel and Beacon head toward chairs being set up for the musicians. As they walk, Daniel's foot catches one of the wires that's snaked across the stage, and he stumbles. A gasp escapes from Carly's mouth, and she has to hold herself back from running over to help. Beacon turns protectively toward Daniel, but he rights himself without actually falling and continues along his way.

A feeling, like a premonition, passes through Carly's mind. She wonders if being with someone blind would always be like this, worrying about a possible mishap. She can't remember ever feeling this way before. As the musicians assemble onstage, Carly finds a seat to one side, a single folding chair that's set off by itself against a wall.

The guy with the ponytail sits down at an electronic keyboard and begins to bang out some jazzy chords. Daniel lifts his saxophone and starts a soft run of scales, so low and mellow that Carly has to strain to hear above the keyboard and a set of drums. When a trumpeter joins in, Daniel's notes blend into a blur of a melody and are no longer distinguishable from the rest. Carly is disappointed. An older man, balding with a fringe of gray hair, is strumming an electric guitar, but his notes are covered by all the rest of what's going on, and Carly wonders why they even need him.

Looking around the room, Carly notices many people who don't look like students: older people and couples who must come in from the neighborhood to hear the music. One very old man, maybe seventy or more, sits by himself up front, close to the keyboard, and nods his head and taps his foot continually to mark the rhythm. Every now and then he lets out an "Oh yeah," and then smiles broadly at one or another of the musicians to show his appreciation.

Daniel's face looks alternately passionate and relaxed as he blows into the mouthpiece of his horn, raising and lowering it gracefully in sync with the rising and falling intensity of the music.

By nine thirty, Carly looks at her watch and realizes she ought to be getting home. She has surprised herself by becoming involved with the music, and the hour here has passed like minutes.

In the back of the room, as she rises to leave, she sees the outline of several men etched against the back wall. In the low light she can't make out their faces, but she can see that they're holding hands on top of the table and looking at each other with their mouths almost close enough to kiss. They stay like this, still and silent, as Carly walks to the door.

Just before leaving, after a last long gaze at Daniel, who plays on and on, Carly glances back once more at the couple. Their faces are suddenly illuminated by the flickering candle. She is stunned when she recognizes her father and his assistant, Edwin. She whirls around and flees as fast as she can.

In her rush back to Broadway, Carly tries to think of gay people she has met, but she can't actually come up with anyone she has known personally. Of course, she has seen guys who are obviously effeminate, walking close to each other or even holding hands, but her father doesn't look at all effeminate and has never struck her as being different in that way.

Now that she thinks about it, Edwin is more the type she thinks of when she thinks of gay men. She wonders if Edwin seduced her father, came on to him at the office one night when no one else was there, and that's when her father figured out he was gay. Carly doubts he thought he was gay when he married her mother, and she can remember a time when they seemed like a normal couple.

Now that Carly knows about her dad and Edwin, she worries about how she should respond. Even if she did let her father know she knows—which she can't imagine doing—she can't say she saw them at the Downunder Café, because she isn't supposed to be there in the first place. And if he did find out that she knows about him and Edwin, would he start acting differently toward her?

Gwen is still absent when Carly lets herself into the apartment and changes quickly out of her clothes and into pajamas. The image of her dad and Edwin holding hands keeps coming back to her. She wonders if her mom knows. This must be the reason she's sad and angry all the time. Carly decides, at least for now, to keep everything the same between her and her father. She can't imagine telling anyone about seeing them, not even Lauren.

CHAPTER SEVEN

s soon as Carly arrives at the Lenskys' on Sunday, Lauren grabs her by the arm and drags her into her room.

"So tell me all about what's going on with your mother's patient. Have you seen him again, the gorgeous blind guy?"

"Yeah, actually, I have. I heard him play jazz sax at Columbia the other night."

"What? Did he invite you?" Lauren plops down on her bed and crosses her legs Indian style. "Tell me! I'm all ears."

"I read in my mother's notebook that he had this gig at a campus nightclub called the Downunder, so I showed up."

"And you introduced yourself, right?"

"I just watched until I had to leave before the set was over. It was cool."

"Do you still have his number from that ad you saw?"

"Yeah, I memorized it," Carly says. "Eight-seven-four-one-eight-zero-four."

Lauren points at the phone. "I dare you."

"Dare me what?"

"Don't be dumb, Carly. I dare you to call." Lauren picks up a piece of charcoal and begins sketching a large, leafy tree on her shiny white Formica dresser top.

"Aren't you gonna get in trouble for drawing on the furniture?"

"It erases," Lauren tells her, and rubs out the sketch.

If Carly could draw as good a tree as the one Lauren has just obliterated, she'd be sure to save it for the rest of her life. Lauren picks up the phone and hands it to Carly.

"I was thinking I'd wait a while."

"What're you scared of? You think he'll hang up on you?"

"It's not that. It's just . . ." Carly doesn't know what else to say.

"You're scared your mother will find out."

"How's she gonna find out? I wouldn't give my real name or anything."

"Then do it, for Chrissake. Just do it. You're always saying you'll do stuff, and then you always wimp out."

"That's not true," Carly protests, but she's beginning to feel cornered. "It's just that I wanna do it when I'm alone."

"Well, pardon me," Lauren says dramatically with a theatrical flourish of a bow, and exits the room, calling back over her shoulder, "I guess I know when I'm not wanted."

Carly turns over the receiver and dials a jumble of numbers. When she hears the recorded announcement that she has reached a number that's out of service, she hangs up and calls out, "You can come back now. He's not home."

"Too bad," Lauren says, and goes over to the dresser. Quick as a flash, she sketches a male nude with an erect penis. "Maybe next time you'll be luckier."

Carly imagines Daniel playing the sax with no clothes on.

"*Papa est là*," Tibou calls in from the kitchen. "*Venez, venez vite. Le dîner est servi.*"

Lauren translates: "My father's home. It's time to eat."

"Aren't you gonna erase that?" Carly asks, pointing at the sketch of the male nude.

"What for?"

Going to Lauren's is one of the things Carly likes best in the world. It feels like traveling to a foreign country, not just three floors down. Tibou speaks French to Lauren and her father, an émigré architect, who speaks Russian to Lauren and her mother. Lauren speaks English to both parents, but sometimes when she's in a contrary mood, she'll yell something at her father in French or curse her mother in Russian.

"It keeps them on their toes," she explains when Carly asks why. Then she translates, "It keeps them on their toes," into Russian and French.

Carly tells her, "You should translate for the United Nations when you grow up," but Lauren flips her shaggy mane of dirty-blond hair out of her eyes and says, "I was born to paint."

She's the only person her age Carly has ever known who knows what she was born to be.

Mr. Lensky designs radically modern homes for rich and famous people. On the refrigerator next to one of Marc's pictures from school, Tibou has posted the cover from an *Architectural Digest* with a photo of his latest house, the home of a well-known sculptor who lives in Southampton. It looks like a triple-layer wedding cake with windows. As Carly enters the kitchen, Marc announces, "It's the first house ever built where every interior and exterior wall is round."

Everyone speaks English to Marc, who refuses to answer to anything else. Marc claims his imaginary friend Ezra, for whom he sets a special place at the table, doesn't understand Russian or French. Ezra even has his own napkin ring, one with a duck's head carved out of wood. When Tibou goes around giving out portions, she make-believe serves Ezra too, tapping a serving spoon on the clean plate at the empty place. During the meal Marc leans over and whispers something at the air where Ezra's head would be.

When Lauren tells him, "It's rude to whisper at the dinner table," Tibou says, "And it's ruder to break a magic spell."

After the main course is cleared, Marc pops up and turns off the light, and Tibou comes back out of the kitchen carrying a birthday cake with candles. "*Bonne anniversaire, ma petite,*" she tells Carly as she sets it down before her on the table and kisses the top of her head.

"You have to make a wish before you blow them out," Marc announces. "And you can't tell anyone what you wished or it won't come true."

Carly feels a lump in her throat forming and is afraid she might cry. She wants to get over the part where everyone's watching her, and so before she even gets a chance to make her wish, she blows the candles out. Everyone claps as Tibou hands her a cake knife and says, "You do zee honors, *ma petite.*"

After dinner, Lauren walks Carly out into the hall and waits with her for the elevator to come. She hands her a little package with gift wrapping and a ribbon on it. "For your birthday, *ma vieille.*"

"Hey, you didn't have to do that," Carly tells her. She feels the lump forming in her throat again and changes the subject. "And I'm not old. I'm only sixteen."

"You can open it later. And *ma vieille* means 'my old friend,' not that you're actually an old person."

Because she doesn't know what else to say, Carly changes the subject again as she holds open the door to the elevator with her foot. "Did you see those creepy photos of homeless people Mr. Laszlo took?"

"Yucko. I bet he gets off on girls changing behind that little screen of his," Lauren says.

That hasn't occurred to Carly, but as she gets on the elevator she tells Lauren, "I bet he does too."

When Carly lets herself in through the back door of her apartment, she finds a note on the refrigerator: *I'm out for the evening and should be home by eleven. Mom.*

Even though her mom was upset that Carly scheduled dinner with the Lenskys, she can't help feeling betrayed that her mother is out doing something else on her birthday. To compensate, Carly helps herself to a quart of ice cream from the freezer.

She's about to head upstairs to her bedroom when she remembers the story Katherine told about the girl who got pregnant using plastic wrap for birth control. She goes over to the cabinet where paper goods are stored, tears off a length of Saran, wraps it around the nozzle of the spray hose in the kitchen sink, and turns the water on full force. Water gushes everywhere, soaking the cabinets and the ceiling and spotting the floral-print paper on the walls.

An hour later, Carly is lying on her bed, holding her stuffed gray squirrel and daydreaming. Lauren's gift of little note cards she made with her own drawings of flowers are spread out on the desk, and the quart of ice cream has melted in a puddle on her bedroom carpet. She's imagining Daniel lying on his back straddling a weight bench, all alone, no clothes, slowly raising and lowering a bar of weights. She begins to touch her breast and then moves her hand downward and rolls over. From downstairs in the foyer, she hears the front door opening and then Gwen calling from below, "Carly? I'm home. Are you there?"

CHAPTER EIGHT

arly's excited when she meets Lauren in the lobby at nine fifteen on Saturday morning. This gives them forty-five minutes to amble leisurely down Fifth Avenue to the Art Students League on West Fifty-Seventh Street to the final spring session of Robert Dahl's figure-painting class.

Even though she doesn't say so, Carly knows Lauren's in love with Robert Dahl. She can tell from the way Lauren acts whenever she's around him, which reminds Carly of the way she feels about Michael Landon from *Little House on the Prairie*.

Robert Dahl is the kindest man Carly has ever known in real life. He wears soft, nappy, unmatched jackets and slacks, plaid shirts, no tie. He's tall and thin and leans toward you like a supple tower when he talks to you about your paintings, even though Carly knows her work is inferior to what everyone around her is doing. Unlike Lauren, Carly knows she wasn't born to paint. But even so, when Robert Dahl sits down to discuss her painting, Carly gets the feeling he has all the time in the world and that her work is as important to him as the Sistine Chapel.

Carly loves the Saturday morning walk downtown and the way Lauren describes the scenery they pass. Looking through

Lauren's eyes, the world grows clearer and keener. Carly sees details—purple shadows beneath green leaves, triangles and trapezoids of space—that she never knew were there. Somewhere high above Manhattan, Lauren shows her the shape of the sky: a slice of azure here, a wedge there. But suddenly Lauren changes the subject and surprises Carly with a question.

"Don't you think Dahl's the type that likes women to come on to him, rather than being the one to start stuff?"

Carly is taken totally off guard.

"I mean, he's obviously the shy and gentle type," Lauren continues, "and I'm just wondering if he'd be more receptive if a woman was the aggressor rather than the other way around."

"Maybe he'd be disgusted and shy away," Carly offers.

"Men aren't *disgusted* by sex, Carly! That's what they want. They just have to figure out how to get it. Sometimes the woman has to help them find the way. At least that's what Tibou says."

"Tibou? You mean your mother talks to you about this stuff?"

"Of course she does. It's part of life, no?"

"It may be part of life, but not a part of life that I can imagine discussing with my mother," Carly admits.

"Well, your mom's American, and Americans are uptight about sex. In Europe, sex is treated like something natural and healthy. Not everyone in the world got fucked up by the Puritans."

When Carly starts laughing, Lauren asks, "What's so funny?"

"It's kind of ironic, don't you think, your using *fucked up* to describe how the Puritans made Americans so inhibited about sex?"

"What I think is that it's obvious you're uncomfortable talking about this."

"I'm not uncomfortable talking about it at all," Carly protests.

"Then what about *doing* it? Don't you think it's time to lose our virginity? Tibou thinks the reason American women are more frigid than French women is 'cause they hold on to their virginity for so long, they lose their natural instinct."

Carly has never been exposed to this theory before, but now that she thinks about it, she wonders if this explains why her parents seem so sad and distant all the time. Maybe the problem is that her mom's frigid and doesn't want to have sex with her dad.

Lauren breaks Carly's train of thought when she asks, "What if I hang back after class today and wait till everyone's out of the studio? I could catch Dahl alone in back where we store our canvases—"

"Lauren! Are you crazy? What if he's not interested in having sex with you?"

"Today's the last class. I wouldn't have to see him again."

"But we'll be taking class again in the fall," Carly says.

Lauren seems impatient when she replies, "The fall's a millennium away. Who knows where we'll be and what we'll be doing."

Carly imagines Lauren coming on to Mr. Dahl, and she imagines him pushing Lauren away and asking what the hell she thinks she's doing. "I'll wait across the street in the art supply shop," Carly offers. "Just in case things don't work out so great."

"Don't be such a pessimist, Carly. Nothing ventured, nothing gained."

"Is that also something Tibou says?"

"You're just a spoilsport, Carly."

"I am not. I'm just being realistic."

"We make our own reality."

"Which sounds totally like Tibou," Carly says, and she and Lauren both break out laughing.

When they arrive at the League, they get their smocks and paint boxes out of their lockers and set up their canvases on easels in Mr. Dahl's studio. Carly started a few weeks ago on a picture of three nuns braving a storm, but she hasn't been able to bring it into focus.

When Mr. Dahl comes around to her easel, he sits down on a stool and says, "Tell me what you're thinking about for this painting, Carly."

He listens attentively, nodding encouragingly as she tries to explain what her painting is about, but she's having trouble concentrating and can't help thinking about what Lauren is planning to do. As Mr. Dahl sits swinging his long legs slowly back and forth, Carly imagines Lauren going up to him in the back of the studio. Will she wrap her arms around him, Carly wonders, and try to kiss him, or maybe she'll try to rub his crotch to excite him that way.

"I have an idea of blending together the nuns' habits to give the impression that all three are one."

In the back of Carly's mind, lodged somewhere in the tangle of thoughts that she knows she hasn't managed to convey in paint, is the concept of God in all things. She just finished reading *The Nun's Story*, and it's very much on her mind.

"I like your idea very much, Carly. How do you think you can convey it pictorially?"

The more words she uses, the longer she speaks, the more certain she becomes that nothing she has achieved on paper resembles her imagined design.

"You've got some good, solid ideas, Carly," Mr. Dahl is saying. "You might want to work out your thoughts in a few charcoal sketches to explore the possibilities."

Carly knows this is Mr. Dahl's gentle way of saying that what she has done so far isn't working. When she looks at her painting, buckling under oozing layers of paint, she sees a blob of blue gray that stands for the sky and a mess of muddy black filling the rest of the canvas and running off onto the surface of the easel.

Carly thinks of the paintings in her apartment, and she suddenly gets an idea that maybe "abstractions" are really botched attempts at painting stuff that doesn't come out right.

That's the other thing Joel does lots of besides work, collecting art: huge, bright oil paintings that are so large they cover up entire walls. When Carly looks at these "abstractions," as Joel calls them, she tries to identify recognizable objects. One canvas in their living room is covered with messy black and blue brushstrokes that she decides must stand for a storm at sea. Another painting, the one in the front foyer, has an enormous grayish-pink mass plunging through a pale blue background onto a beige streak of foreground. Carly's convinced this one's a gigantic bird crash-landing on a beach.

"The artist doesn't necessarily have a real object in mind," Joel explains when Carly voices her interpretations.

"Then how does he know what to put where?" she asks.

"Artists just know," Joel tells her, but she's still not satisfied.

It makes her feel left out and lonely to stand before these larger-than-life-size inventions of some alien imagination. How can she trust these images that contain hidden messages, the meaning of which she can never know for sure? Carly much prefers pictures of people or boats or still lifes of fruits and flowers. She's glad she and Lauren get to draw and paint stuff that looks like what it really is.

When class ends, Carly quickly stores her canvas in the rack at the back of the room, packs up her paint box and smock, and stashes them in her locker. She sees Lauren still at her easel, taking her time, and when she catches her eye, she flashes a hand sign for OK and points across the street. Lauren flashes back the same sign and then makes Carly cringe with embarrassment as she pokes the index finger of her other hand through it to make the gross gesture guys make to symbolize intercourse.

In the art store, Carly especially loves the tubes of Grumbacher paints and makes a point each week of adding several to her collection. The names of the colors fascinate her: ochre, which is mustardy yellow; cadmium red, which reminds her of the earth; cerulean blue, which sounds like the closest thing in paint to pure peace. The acrylics are extremely expensive—as much as five dollars for a small tube, twice as much for the large ones—but their price confers value, and they feel like weighty little treasures in her hand.

After only ten minutes, Lauren comes up to Carly from behind, puts her arms around her, and covers Carly's eyes with her hands. "Guess who?" she says, and Carly whirls around, surprised.

"What happened? How come you're here so soon?"

"He ducked out before I got a chance. He must have had someplace he needed to go, 'cause he usually hangs around longer."

"Well, that solves that problem!" Carly is relieved, even though she can tell that Lauren's disappointed.

"Guess where Dahl lives?" Lauren asks as they leave the art store.

"I don't have a clue," Carly tells her, pretending not to care.

"I looked him up in the phone book." Lauren sounds pleased with herself. "And he lives in the Village at ten and a half St. Luke's Place."

"How can anyone live at an address like ten and a half?" Carly wants to know. "Doesn't it have to be a whole number?"

"Wanna go see for ourselves?" Lauren asks casually, as though she hasn't been working on this plan for days.

"You mean, go there? And just look?" It seems like a strange thing to do.

"Why not?"

She can tell that Lauren is already counting on her saying yes. "Do you have any plans for the afternoon?"

"I'll have to call my mother. She expects me home to study for finals," Carly tells her, fabricating the excuse she'll give for what she'll be doing.

"Here's a quarter." Lauren fishes in her pocket and comes up with the coin. "And there's a pay phone at the League."

They cross back over Fifty-Seventh Street, and Carly calls Gwen from the lobby phone. She tells her there's a lecture at the Museum of Modern Art on Vincent van Gogh, and that lots of kids from her art class are going to hear it. Carly knows Gwen likes it when she does things with groups of kids. It makes her think Carly's popular and normal. Carly figures a Van Gogh lecture is a safe bet: first, because Gwen is likely to approve, and second, because she recently finished *Lust for Life*. If Gwen asks any questions later about what was said, Carly will be able to come up with all sorts of tidbits.

As Carly and Lauren leave the building, they walk down the hall. Everyone's hanging around in blue jeans and big white, paint-covered button-down shirts, looking like Jackson Pollock splatter paintings. They pass the double studio where Monsieur and Madame Laliberté teach the male and female nude classes. In Madame Laliberté's room, the same fat female nude from last week is sitting up on the platform, drinking coffee and smoking a cigarillo during a break. Next door, in Monsieur's studio, Carly gets a full frontal view of the male nude model in that little string thing they wear. The image of her dad and Edwin comes to mind, and because Carly doesn't want to let her thoughts go any further, she turns her head and walks past as fast as she can.

Just before leaving the building, Lauren detours to her locker and takes out her paint box and smock.

"They said returning students can leave their stuff till after the summer," Carly tells her.

Lauren clips back, "Yeah, well, some of us are actually planning to paint during the summer."

"You mean those of us who aren't being parked at camp in Colorado?"

As they head for Fifth Avenue, Carly asks Lauren, "Why would anyone want to paint a fat thing like that female nude in Madame Laliberté's studio?"

"Artists find beauty in everything," Lauren says, "like Van Gogh's old shoes. You can tell your mom they talked about that at the lecture."

Now Carly wishes she could take back what she said about the fat model.

Carly and Lauren ride the Fifth Avenue bus all the way downtown. It's like Mallory might have sounded, Carly imagines, climbing Mount Everest, or Christopher Columbus discovering the New World, when the Washington Square Arch looms up before them and Lauren declares, "Hail Greenwich Village! We've arrived!"

The buildings in the Village are all much lower than the buildings uptown, and the streets are narrower and lined with trees and angled in all sorts of improbable, irregular ways. It takes them nearly an hour to find St. Luke's Place. They cross back and forth through Washington Park half a dozen times before they're directed to what seems more like a village lane than an actual street. There are no apartment buildings like the one Carly and Lauren live in uptown, just a row of private houses, each different from the others, with stone steps in front leading down to the tree-lined sidewalk and a pretty little park across the street. It feels like they're in a foreign city, like postcards of Paris, where everything is small and quaint.

Number ten and a half is a deep-red brick building with flower boxes in the first-floor windows. It juts out slightly beyond the two houses that surround it, and a big, furry marmalade cat sits licking its paws on the top step. Shutters are closed behind a second-story window that could be a bedroom.

"What if he comes home while we're standing here?" Carly asks Lauren, half frozen in fear and half thrilled at the possibility.

"What if he's already home?" Lauren sounds like she thinks this might actually be so. "He could've gotten home hours ago if he left right after class."

"What if he comes out and sees us?" Carly asks, convinced now that Robert Dahl is lurking somewhere within the red brick walls, possibly even peeking out from one of the windows and watching them watch his house.

"We'll just look surprised and say we were walking by."

Carly is more and more certain that Lauren has been working on this plan for ages.

Suddenly, they spot movement behind one of the windows on the lower floor, and before they can react, the front door opens and a woman and a small child walk out onto the landing. She's short and young with jet-black hair cut close to her head. She's wearing large silver hoop earrings and a dark cotton skirt with a big, baggy men's sweater on top. Carly figures out right away that the sweater—it looks soft and nappy—belongs to her husband, Robert Dahl, and that the child, who looks like a girl but Carly can't be sure—it wears bright green corduroy coveralls—is theirs.

"Let's get going," Carly mutters under her breath, but Lauren stands absolutely still, unwilling to move.

The woman and child are unaware of them. She takes its hand and starts down toward the street, the little child catching one foot up to the other before taking each new step.

"We go see Daddy now," Carly hears the woman tell the child, "and take the big bus."

"Let's go, Lauren," Carly says, pulling on Lauren's arm now. "We're out of here!"

And before they know where they're going, they're running like the wind down St. Luke's Place and around the angles and alleyways of Village streets that lead them to the fountain in Washington Square Park. They collapse breathless and convulse in laughter. The weather's warm for early May, and people all around are acting like it's summer. A group of kids have taken off their shoes and socks and are sitting on the edge of the fountain, dipping their bare feet in the water.

"Boy, that was a close call," Lauren says when they finally stop laughing.

"What do you mean, close call?" Carly asks. "Didn't you hear what she said to the kid? They were going to meet its daddy, so Dahl wasn't there."

"He can't have a little kid like that." Lauren sounds annoyed, maybe a little angry.

"Why not?" Carly asks. "He's not so old."

"Yeah, I know, but he'd have to be married." Lauren may be blushing, but it's hard to tell since she's flushed from all the running. "I mean, most people with kids are married and all."

"Well, who'd you think that woman was, his mother?"

"I hadn't thought of that," Lauren says sadly, and Carly, too, feels deflated that the bubble has burst on Lauren's fantasy of having a personal relationship with Mr. Dahl.

"You wanna go somewhere and grab a bite to eat?" Lauren asks, clearly wanting to change the subject.

"Come to think of it, I'm starving," Carly tells her, becoming aware for the first time in hours that she hasn't consumed anything all day but a glass of orange juice before leaving for the Art Students League.

They walk a couple of blocks east of Washington Square Park and stop at the first coffee shop they come to. Lauren orders a Greek salad and iced tea, and Carly orders a bacon cheeseburger with fries and a chocolate shake.

"You'll get fat if you eat that way," Lauren tells her when the waitress brings their food.

"Get fat? I think it's already too late to worry about getting fat."

"You're actually getting kind of skinny. Tibou says you're losing your baby fat."

It's Carly's turn to change the subject. She asks Lauren about a boy she has been dating named Elliott.

"He's OK," Lauren tells her. "Beginning to pressure me about sleeping with him. It's not that I care particularly either way, but I'm thinking he's not worth losing my virginity."

Carly tries to look unfazed by what Lauren has just said, but she's shocked.

Before she can think of how to respond, Lauren says, "Hey, how about that blind guy your mother sees? I saw him in the elevator the other day with his dog. Are you gonna finally make a move, or what?"

Carly is still reacting to what Lauren said about Elliott pressuring her to sleep with him. She tries to visualize Elliott, whom she has met several times hanging out at Lauren's: a tense, greasy-haired boy with a nervous eye blink and fingernails bitten to the quick. Lauren claims he's an intellectual, but Carly has never heard him say more than two words at a time. Usually he just looks anxious and impatient, as though he's waiting to get Lauren alone.

"Do you want to sleep with him?" Carly asks.

"The blind guy? Sure. He's hot."

"No, I mean Elliott. Do you think you'll sleep with him?"

"I dunno," Lauren says, popping a french fry from Carly's plate in her mouth. "I might. But I'd better decide soon, 'cause we're moving to California."

Carly has just taken a bite of her cheeseburger when Lauren says this, and she almost chokes.

"You're doing what?"

"We're moving. We have to. My father is being transferred to Los Angeles."

"How can you move? You live here and go to school here . . ."

"Like that matters," Lauren says. "Tibou says there are houses and schools in California too."

"So your mom wants to move?"

"I didn't say she *wants* to move. We have to move, so she's doing what she always does, making the best of things."

Carly suddenly realizes why Lauren didn't leave her paint box and smock in the locker at the League. "I can't believe it, Lauren. What are we gonna do?"

"We can always write letters, I suppose, although that's not much fun. Maybe you can come visit during holidays."

It begins to sink in that Lauren and her family are really moving, and all the energy and excitement of the day slips away. If Lauren isn't going to be there too, Carly decides she won't take Dahl's class in the fall. Sadness is seeping into Carly's mood, and she feels on the verge of breaking down in tears. A big, heavy tear hovers on her eyelid before falling onto a puddle of ketchup on her plate. Carly really doesn't want Lauren to see her cry and feels irrationally angry that she didn't tell her about the move in time for Carly to take her paint box and smock too.

When Lauren notices how sad and quiet Carly has become, she reaches across the table and covers Carly's hand with her own. "I know. It sucks. I'm gonna miss you too," Lauren says, before changing the subject really fast.

"By the way, I liked your nuns very much. They reminded me of that book my mother used to read me, the one about the little French girl named Madeleine"—Lauren pronounces the name with a perfect French accent—"who lives at a convent school and always does everything all in a row with all the other little girls who wear the same uniforms. Hey!" Lauren perks up. "Just like you and all the Baxter bitches."

Carly ignores the insult. "I read those books too, but mine were in English, and her name was Madeline."

On their way to the uptown bus, Lauren brings up Elliott again. "I guess I'd better do something about sleeping with Elliott. Tibou has offered to take me to her gynecologist to get fitted."

"To do what?"

"Get fitted. For a diaphragm. She says I'm old enough to take responsibility."

Carly can barely believe what she's hearing, that someone's mother is actually encouraging them to get birth control. But she's beginning to realize it must be true that French people are way more liberal about sex than uptight Americans.

Still, Carly thinks that if Lauren's going to sleep with someone, the person should be much better than Elliott. She imagines Lauren with someone mature and serious who appreciates her talent. Someone like Robert Dahl. Since Lauren's an artist, Carly figures, for double indemnity she should sleep with one as well. Carly gets the feeling that it's different, not just about sex, with Robert Dahl and the woman with the cropped jet-black hair and the baggy sweater.

The sadness over Lauren's leaving gets worse when Carly gets home. She doesn't mention it to Gwen, because that would make it more real. That night before she falls asleep, Carly imagines Monsieur and Madame Laliberté from the Art Students League making passionate love, and she knows, just knows, that's what it would be like with Lauren and Robert Dahl. Just before dozing off, the image of Daniel lying nude lifting weights swims into her mind. Suddenly, she's not sleepy anymore, and Carly rolls over, pushes the pillow down between her legs, and imagines climbing on top of Daniel and rubbing up against his erection.

CHAPTER NINE

At eight o'clock on Wednesday morning, Carly is dressed and ready for school. Instead of books, her knapsack is packed with a change of clothes and a pad of paper. Just as she's heading for the door, Gwen catches up with her and asks if she has had something for breakfast.

"I grabbed a bagel to eat on the way," Carly lies, and before Gwen has a chance to object, Carly flees into the hall.

She closes the door hard behind her and punches the down button on the elevator three times in quick succession. Her heart is beating so hard she can feel blood pumping in her chest.

Once inside the elevator, Carly presses the button for the second floor instead of the lobby, and when the elevator stops, she gets out and ducks into the back hallway, where no one ever goes except to set out trash. She goes down half a flight to the little landing area where the stairs turn the corner and quickly changes out of her uniform into the jeans and turtleneck she stuffed in her knapsack before leaving.

It's gusty and cold outside, the kind of day that reminds Carly of the damp, wintry way kids smell when they come in from playing hard in the park. Little puffs of foggy breath come out of her mouth as she walks, triggering the urge for a cigarette. She huddles in a doorway and strikes three matches before she lights up and then drags deeply several times in a row, fast, because the number 4 bus is coasting into the Ninety-Sixth Street stop.

A group of kids from Cathedral School—the name is printed on their book bags and uniforms—are talking loudly and joking around at the back of the bus. One of them, a girl with silky shoulder-length brown hair that she keeps running her hand through to sweep it off her face, is telling a story about a kid who got into trouble at school.

"When Mr. Dinkle came over and told him to stop hanging around in the hall outside his room," she informs her friends, who are spellbound in admiration, "Scott goes, 'Hey, man, chill,' and then Mr. Dinkle really loses it and screams at him, 'You get your smart ass straight to the principal's office!' and everyone hanging around, including Lisa Cavalleri, whose father's on the board, is taking in every word."

This girl really annoys Carly. What she's saying is so ordinary and stupid, and the way she's talking, as though what she's saying is the most important thing in the world, rankles her. And the way she stops talking every couple of words and throws her hair off her face while the other kids just sit there waiting for her to go on—it's so overly dramatic. Carly can't believe how everyone, including the other passengers, are watching this girl's every move and hanging on every word she's broadcasting loud enough for the entire bus to hear. Then Carly realizes that she's watching and listening too, and she decides to look away and tune out. It's her own silent protest, but she'll be damned if she's going to allow this self-centered little bitch to get everyone's attention.

When the bus stops at 110th and Amsterdam, the Cathedral kids descend in a pack and clamor out onto the street: a continuous flow of navy blue and gray and white with heads with different-color hair streaking down and out and away. As the girl passes, Carly catches her eye and sneers at her. She wouldn't be such a self-confident show-off, Carly thinks, if she were all by herself.

As the bus rounds the corner of ll0th and Riverside, Carly feels herself getting tense. She's only a few stops away from Columbia and then a quick walk to Daniel's apartment. A special sensation knots her stomach, a twist of pain that tugs at her from inside and sends a taste like the aftermath of vomit up to the bottom of her throat.

The image of Gwen's tense and worried face before leaving the house comes back to her, and it's joined by the image of Ms. Harrington. A collage of the two faces forms in Carly's mind, and mentally she tears it into tiny pieces and tosses it out over the sparkling blue water of the Hudson River.

The sense of control she gets from making the choice not to go to school, her own school, today, gives her a surge of pleasure. She feels all-powerful, as though she could leap across the river in one bound, or spring up into the cloudless blue sky.

At ll6th Street, Carly gets off the bus and climbs the hill toward Broadway. She remembers her way perfectly, as though she has walked this route not twice before but dozens of times. In less than ten minutes, she's arrived. Lighting a cigarette, she leans against a car and takes up a position outside Butler Hall. It's only eight twenty in the morning, and Carly has the entire day with nothing to do but wait for Daniel. A steady stream of traffic flows out of the building: some young people whom Carly assumes are students, and some other older men and women who are obviously headed for work.

By nine fifteen the flow of traffic has slowed down, and just as Carly is beginning to worry that Daniel left before she got there, the front door to Butler Hall opens and Beacon comes out with Daniel holding his harness. With amazing precision, the ritual of Beacon urinating and defecating in the gutter is reenacted. Only this time he chooses a spot on the other side of the entrance, so Carly doesn't bother holding her breath for fear of being detected by the dog.

Just as Daniel is connecting up with Beacon's harness again, a man in a trench coat leaves Butler Hall and heads toward Amsterdam Avenue. When he brushes by Daniel, he pats him on the back and calls out, a little extra loud, as though the blind are hard of hearing too, "Hi, Dan, how's it going? Frank Guinness here."

"Hey, Frank, how ya doing?" Dan calls back cheerily. Frank is already a couple paces beyond him.

"Great, Dan, just great," he shouts back, sounding pleased with himself.

Carly gets the feeling the guy thinks he just did his good deed for the day.

As she follows Daniel and Beacon, who start walking slowly west toward Amsterdam, Carly thinks about Daniel's voice. She heard him speak once or twice before to the little girl at the bus stop that first day, and sometimes he exchanges greetings with the doormen under her building as he leaves. It's a surprisingly self-confident voice, Carly thinks, for a person who can't see. If she just heard the voice and didn't know that the person speaking was blind or in any way disabled, she wouldn't have a clue that anything was wrong.

Carly trails Daniel as he navigates south along Amsterdam Avenue, turning west at the corner by the journalism school on 116th Street, where he and Beacon cross over to the rear entrance to the Columbia campus. Carly wonders if Daniel has any difficulty getting around. He seems to manage so easily, as though he knows as well as any sighted person what lies in his path and where the way is leading.

Once within the gate and safely on campus, Daniel and Beacon pick up speed. Beacon is obviously as used to it here as the students hanging around on the stone steps of the formal-looking buildings.

It will be easy, Carly decides as she looks around and sees a universe of every imaginable type of person going to and from the various buildings. Every one of them looks like they belong here, like they have a reason, made just for them, to be here in this place that's not like any place Carly has ever been.

There are African students with long, colorful robes and fancy headgear; Indian women wearing saris and men with turbans wrapped like beehives around their heads; male and female students dressed alike in all black with heavy black shoes with shiny metal sprockets to hold the laces. There are guys and girls who look no older than Carly, and men and women who could be someone's grandparents. There are mothers pushing babies in strollers and people walking dogs. Every few hundred feet Carly passes a table where serious-looking men and women are arguing various causes and handing out literature: students against apartheid in South Africa, others in favor of legalizing drugs, pro-abortion and women's rights, an anti-Noriega table, support for the homeless, a table where you can sign a petition to the mayor to do more for AIDS victims.

Daniel and Beacon wend their way through the maze of activity until they arrive at a broad, low building with *Dodge Hall* printed on the stone over the entranceway. Beacon avoids a ramp made out of wood, jury-rigged in compliance with handicap regulations, in favor of the stone steps. Once inside, Beacon leads Daniel toward the elevators, where several students and a man in a tweed jacket with elbow patches stand waiting. Carly slips into the group, standing so close to Daniel that the sleeve of her jacket brushes up against his arm. A gust of breath escapes from her mouth, like steam from a teakettle, and a trickle of excitement reverberates throughout her body.

"Hi, Professor Pietro," a girl standing on the other side of Daniel says, smiling up at the man.

"Good morning, Miss Morningstar," the professor replies in a foreign accent. "I'm looking forward to reading your paper on Puccini. I hope you'll get a chance to see the production of *La Bohème* that starts next week at the Met."

Carly decides the professor's accent must be Italian.

"A bunch of us are going," the young woman responds. "We've got nosebleed tickets way up in Seventh Heaven."

Carly feels left out of what she figures must be an in-joke when the professor and some of the other students break out laughing.

When the elevator door opens, they pack in and ride up to the fifth floor. Carly follows along with the group, which heads down the hall toward a classroom already half filled with students. Daniel takes an aisle seat toward the front of the room, and Carly sits diagonally to the right behind him. Beacon curls up in a tight black ball at Daniel's feet, cushioning his jaw on his crossed front paws, not stirring at all except to lift his eyes to look up as students file by. The dog seems sad when he does this, and Carly wonders how much he can possibly understand about Daniel's being blind and different from all these other people.

There must be thirty or forty people in the room by the time the professor begins his lecture, and no one seems to be noticing Carly. After the first few nervous minutes of trying to look like she belongs, she begins to relax.

You don't have to do anything special, she realizes, to look the part of one of the students. Most of them sit listening to the lecture and taking lots of notes. Daniel doesn't take notes, but Carly sees the small black plastic box that he has placed on the arm of his seat to record the professor. A few of the students just listen and don't seem to be writing anything at all, but since Carly doesn't want to take any chances of arousing suspicion, she pulls out her pad of paper and scrawls a note every now and then.

The professor, who's tall and thin and wears round metal-rimmed glasses, is discoursing on the role of music in seventeenth- and eighteenth-century European life. He speaks slowly, pronouncing each word deliberately in his thick Italian accent, as though he's trying to make it easy for students to take down his words.

"It was not like today in this country, for example," he says with a smile that forecasts a punch line. "There was no television, no video, no cinema."

All of his short *i* sounds are pronounced "*ee*." The professor looks around the room expectantly, and a few students smile or laugh obligingly.

"Not even the radio."

He pauses dramatically, leaning with one arm against the blackboard, his palm spread wide, leaving the necessary amount of time before pouncing verbally on his audience like a trial lawyer with just the right morsel of evidence to persuade a reluctant jury. "Instead"—the professor is smiling even more broadly—"they had music."

The entire room, including Daniel, roars with laughter. Carly isn't sure if the class is laughing because of some special significance to what the professor has just said, or if they're laughing because the professor pronounced the word "*museek*," giving equal emphasis to both syllables.

Encouraged by the students' favorable response, the professor decides to tell a story from his personal life, a special aside not related to his lecture.

"You don't need to write this down," he tells the class, waving his hand dismissively.

Students all around the room lay down their pens. Daniel doesn't change the setting of his recorder, which he keeps running just as before.

The story is about the professor's flight from Europe. As a very young boy at the outbreak of World War II, en route from Italy to freedom abroad, his father took the whole family through Paris to see the Mona Lisa.

"My father was worried," the professor tells the class, "that by the end of the war the Louvre might be destroyed."

The students are listening with rapt attention. Beacon's gentle snoring is the only sound beside the professor's voice.

"There was a war going on, and we had to rush. It was like seeing the Louvre on roller skates. The Mona Lisa smiled at me, but she smiled fast."

The class erupts in laughter.

Carly is imagining the professor's parents. The father has thick gray hair and a bushy mustache. The mother is small and stocky, dark haired and Mediterranean looking, and she wears a scarf wound around her head and tied under her chin. Carly pictures the professor as a thin, intense little boy between them, holding a hand of each, as he rolls on skates through the Louvre.

And then Carly remembers herself, a tired, bored girl of ten, walking listlessly with her own parents through those same galleries when she went to Paris. It hits her like a time warp boomeranging back at her, and she's filled with longing for another chance to be born all over again in someone else's skin, in another self to different parents and a completely changed life. She can feel the breeze against her skin and the thrill of speeding to new sights and sounds. She sees herself in a long, loose garment with a high ruffled collar, like the robes women and children wear in Renaissance paintings. Her face is the face of the *Mona Lisa* as she skates smiling through the cool marble corridors of the Louvre.

"Since this is our final class of the semester," the professor is saying as he gathers his papers on the podium, "I want to wish all of you a good summer season, and may it be filled with the sound of music!"

Carly is amazed when the students rise to their feet and begin clapping wildly. Not wanting to look like she doesn't know what's going on, Carly gets up too, and applauds Professor Pietro along with Daniel and all the rest.

CHAPTER TEN

I t's ten o'clock the last night before camp. Still not having packed her duffel, Carly lies on her bed holding her furry gray squirrel. The list of required clothes and supplies is on her desk with a Magic Marker, but she hasn't crossed off a single thing by the time Gwen comes in to check on her progress.

"Hey, what's up, Carly? It's late, and you have to be up early to meet the camp train in the morning."

Carly rolls over and faces the wall. "I don't want to go to camp."

"We've been over this, Carly, and a decision has been made that you're going to camp this summer."

"Your decision has been made." Carly's voice has grown louder and firmer, and she sits up on her bed and tucks her squirrel behind her pillow.

Gwen goes over to Carly's dresser, on which piles of clothes are stacked, and starts putting them in the empty duffel.

"Leave my stuff alone!" Carly is screaming now, and in a minute her father appears in the doorway.

"What's the matter? What's going on?" Joel asks.

"Carly's staging an eleventh-hour strike," Gwen announces.

"But we don't have time for this anymore, so let's get you packed up."

As Gwen puts more things in the duffel, Carly jumps off the bed and runs over to stop her. She grabs her mother's arm and yanks it away, dislodging a pile of shirts and shorts, which tumble onto the floor.

Joel rushes over to pull Carly off Gwen. "Hey, slow down there, Squirrelkin. Your mom's only trying to be helpful."

"I am not your fucking Squirrelkin, and Mom is not helping me!"

"Carly," Gwen intervenes in her calm but menacing voice that she uses to reestablish control, "one way or another, you are getting on the train tomorrow morning and going to camp this summer. You can spend tonight throwing yet another temper tantrum and acting out like a little child, or you can get your packing organized and over with so you can get some sleep before your travels. It's your choice."

"It's not my choice!" Carly is screaming at full throttle now, and then just as suddenly as her anger has erupted, she slides down on the floor, holds her head in her hands, and begins to sob loudly, gasping for breath and sounding as though she's about to choke to death.

Gwen whirls around and leaves the room, but Joel goes over to Carly and sits down beside her on the floor.

"Hey? It's me. Your dad," Joel says in a gentle, soft voice as he rubs Carly's back.

Carly's sobbing lets up slightly, but she shakes her head back and forth, as though she's signaling no to Joel's overture.

"Give me a chance, Squirrel—" He stops himself before finishing. "I mean, Carly, give your dad a chance."

Thoughts of her father and Edwin are whirling around in Carly's mind. Part of her wants to lash out and accuse Joel of his betrayal, and part of her wants to sink into his arms and let herself be cuddled like the little girl she has become again.

Carly leans her head on her father's shoulder, and in between crying and sucking up her tears she tells him, "Oh, Dad, everything's ruined. Nothing's the way it's supposed to be."

"There, there. You'll feel better in the morning when you've had some sleep. How about you and I finish up the packing together? It'll make it go faster. What do you say?"

Carly doesn't say anything but begins to unfold herself from being curled up on the floor. Joel stands up and holds out his hands to her. Carly places her feet on top of his, the way she used to do as a little girl, and Joel pulls her up and into his arms for a hug. But the hugging part is too much for her—she keeps thinking of her dad and Edwin—and she pulls away.

"I can handle this by myself," Carly tells her dad, who looks around the room and nods his head continually, as though quantifying the amount of work that needs to be done.

"You sure you've got this, Carly? I'm here to help if you need me."

"I'll take care of it," Carly tells him, and Joel finally retreats and leaves her alone.

By midnight, Carly has pretty much finished the packing, and just as she gets into bed, she hears the rising murmur of voices coming through the wall from her parents' room. As she dozes off to sleep, Carly picks up occasional words, but mostly she hears a dull, familiar din of anger and accusation passing between her mother and father.

Carly gets more and more depressed the farther west they go and the longer the train trip to Colorado takes. She keeps trying to retrieve the details of the fight her parents were having as she was falling asleep last night, and she can't help feeling that she's being sent away because they don't want her around while they're having problems. Based on the few things she overheard through the wall, Carly thinks her mom suspects her dad of being unfaithful, but she guesses her mom doesn't have a clue about him and Edwin.

Carly can't exactly bring herself to think of her father as homosexual, since he obviously had sex with her mother for her to be born, which technically makes her dad "bi," not gay. She has heard that French people are very tolerant of homosexuals, and she wonders if Tibou thinks being gay or bi is natural and healthy too, the way she thinks sex between men and women is. But when Carly thinks of Edwin, who has always seemed cold and creepy, she can't imagine anyone wanting to have sex with him.

Carly tries to conjure up what it would be like to do stuff with a girl, but when Lauren comes to mind, she remembers that the Lenskys are moving to California at the end of the summer, just when she'll be getting home from camp, and sadness so deep sets in that she can't concentrate on anything else.

Carly has never ridden on a sleeper train before, and she passes the time by studying how the compartment works. The way the seats make up as beds and all the compact, secret storage places fascinate her. According to its glossy twelve-page brochure and the camp consultant lady who came to visit the Kleins, Red Soil Ranch Camp claims to be an "authentic pioneer American experience," and riding the railroad west is part of the package.

The other two girls who share Carly's compartment couldn't care less about how it's designed. They're both a year older, wear lipstick and eye makeup, read romance novels, and have been to Red Soil Ranch Camp before. They also have something substantial to fill out their stretchy white bras that they hang conspicuously on the clothes hooks at night when they change for bed, right out in the open where the porter can see them.

Serena Sneed is the first girl Carly has ever met who wears jeans with a pearl necklace, both at the same time. She cuffs the short sleeves on her nothing-special white blouse and gets the collar to stand up instead of lying flat. Jill Roth wears black tights, no underpants, and a white T-shirt with blue letters that spell out "Yale Sucks" across the front. "My brother got rejected," she explains when Serena asks, "but he's sort of schmucky anyway."

Carly is wearing khaki Bermuda shorts and a red-and-blue-striped Izod shirt, an outfit Gwen sent up from Bloomingdale's, and brand-new tennis shoes and socks. Serena and Jill wear suede moccasins, no socks, and shave their long, lean legs in the oval metal sink on the wall.

When the camp chaperone comes through and calls for lights out, Carly crawls into bed in one of the two upper berths and draws the little half curtain to make it private. She leaves the shade up so she can watch out the window and see the factories and towns fly by. Jill and Serena each have their own lower berths on opposite sides of the compartment, but they visit back and forth, and even though she doesn't really think it's happening, Carly imagines them making out together.

Now that she's heading away from home, Carly realizes she won't be able to keep track of her parents' moods and behaviors. She can't gauge how things are going and sense if her mom has suspicions about Joel and what's going on with Edwin. Eight weeks away at camp in Colorado seems like an eternity. Anything could happen, and how would she know? The farther they go from where they started, the later it gets into the night, the more homesick and anxious Carly feels.

Carly remembers the summer she was twelve and was sent away to Camp Roundelay in Maine for a month. Mostly she remembers feeling homesick during the day and freezing cold at night, when she slept in a bunk with a bunch of other twelve-years-old on cots with blankets so thin you had to wear sweatshirts and hats to bed at night.

When she returned to New York, her bedroom was entirely redecorated. Instead of her white wood bed with the drawer underneath where she kept stuffed animals and dolls, she came home to two studio couches with fitted black covers and matching bolsters. Every night she had to remove the bolsters and unzip the cover before going to bed. When Carly complained and said she wished she could have her old bed back again, her mom told her she was too big for little girl furniture and that the new stuff was very grown-up.

Carly hears Serena and Jill speaking in low voices to one another, and the last thing she remembers before finally falling off to sleep, just as dawn is lighting up the countryside outside her window, is a burst of giggles and a hushed "Shhh, she'll hear us . . ."

When the train reaches Colorado, they transfer to a bus and ride half a day until they get to Red Soil Ranch on the outskirts of a tiny town called Carbondale. They arrive at the end of the afternoon, and there's only enough time to dump their luggage in their assigned bunks before hiking up the hill to the main house for dinner. Right away, Carly starts making mental lists of complaints to convince her parents to let her come home.

Dear Mom and Dad,

I know you're going to think I'm exaggerating about how truly horrible Red Soil Ranch is, but you have to believe me that if the authorities ever found out how badly it's run, they'd close this place down in a heartbeat.

There are no organized or "structured" activities, and other than having to show up for inedible meals and shoveling horse shit, there's nothing to do. The bunks are filthy, and because there's a water shortage, we're only allowed one shower a week. The food is all fattening, high-cholesterol stuff with no fresh fruit or vegetables.

Please, please do not make me spend the summer in this hellhole. Can you please, please let me come home? I promise I'll be more responsible about doing chores and getting my work done.

Love, Carly

Licking closed the envelope, Carly begins to feel better and more energized. Warming to the subject of how much she hates camp, she settles down with a yellow pad and expands her litany of complaints.

Dear Lauren,

Red Soil Ranch Camp is beyond unbearable. I can't believe my mother made me come here. It has to be the worst place I've ever been in my life.

My bunkmates are total and complete freaks. Mary Ellen Brewster comes from Red Oak, Iowa—does such a place even exist?—and Molly Meisel comes from some suburb of Cleveland. Mary Ellen's hair is so light it's practically white. She wears it pulled back in a long braid that accentuates her skinny face and her pale eyes. Is it possible they're actually pink? She reminds me of the albino guinea pig in the science lab at school.

Molly got accepted by mistake 'cause her parents falsified the required medical report so the camp wouldn't know she was born without big toes and only has sealed-over stubs for thumbs. There's no way she can function normally and do all the physical stuff we have to do at this place. She practically can't button her own blouse—and forget about tying shoelaces!

Mary Ellen's totally hung up on religion, and every night before bed she gets down on her knees, makes a little tent with her hands, and says prayers. "Lordy be" is her favorite expression.

During a big storm when lightning and thunder were keeping everyone awake, Mary Ellen told us about her "visions." She described insane stuff like seeing angels on her shoulder and the devil at the bottom of her bed.

Molly is only about five feet tall and has short mousy brown hair that makes her look like a fat little boy. She isn't exactly retarded, but she's extremely babyish for her age. She cries when anyone teases her, screams so loud you can hear her up and down the bunk line when she gets angry, and rebels against camp rules and regulations by staging sit-down strikes. Her parents have to be nuts to send such a kid to a camp like this. But like my mom they probably didn't have a clue about how badly run this place is.

My counselor goes to Queens College. Her name's Rhona and she comes from Roslyn, so everyone calls her Rhona from Roslyn and imitates her Long Island accent behind her back. She's over six feet tall and there's a rumor she has an extra Y chromosome. She dyes her hair shoe-polish black and wears tons of black eyebrow pencil, black eyeliner—above and below her eyes—black mascara, and black tights. Even when she rides horses.

The counselors are supposed to sleep in our bunks, but Rhona never does. Every night at lights out she takes a sleeping bag from under her bed, grabs a flashlight, and warns us if there's any trouble she'll personally see to having us murdered in the morning. Molly gets hysterical whenever Rhona does this, and I have to explain that this is just something she says but not something she really means. Molly keeps crying anyway.

*How's Vermont? And what happened with Elliott before
you left? Write me soon 'cause I'm going crazy here in this
hellhole!*

Love, Carly

Although she doesn't like to make it obvious, Carly actually feels sorry for Molly. She can't help thinking about how
hard everything is for her and how ill-equipped she is to deal
with practically everything that goes on. When no one else
is around, Carly makes a special effort to be nice to her and
to help her with little stuff like buttoning up and tying her
shoelaces. But because she realizes it makes Molly feel self-conscious in front of other kids, Carly does this only when they're
alone.

Carly doesn't really like Molly all that much or think of her
as an actual friend, but sometimes when she's helping her with
things Molly has trouble with, like brushing her hair, she kind of
make-believes that Molly's a younger sister. Carly thinks of Lauren, who doesn't act nice to her brother Marc most of the time,
but when he needs something or when Tibou reminds Lauren
that she has to help her younger brother, Lauren steps up and
does what's needed.

A whole week goes by before Carly gets a card in her cubby
with a photo of rolling green hills postmarked from Vermont.
She turns it over and reads the brief text: *Got your letter from
hell. Ditch Colorado and come to Cabot.* Lauren has made a pencil
sketch of a black-and-white cow with a smiling face and signed
her name the way artists do in the lower right corner.

Nothing arrives from her mom or dad, but she is handed one
more little handmade envelope with Carly's name and address
in Lauren's handwriting. Inside is a torn-off piece of paper on
which Lauren has scribbled:

Hey Carly, sorry I forgot to tell you I slept with Elliott. We just did it once, the last night before I left for Vermont. I mean, we did it a few times, but all in one night. It was cool, but of course I'm not in love with him, so it doesn't mean anything. Hang in there. Nothing lasts forever, especially not virginity. I'm glad I don't have to get rid of THAT anymore.

Even though Lauren finally answered her question about Elliott, it doesn't feel fair that she hasn't bothered to react to any of the descriptions about camp that Carly took so much time and trouble to write. She is jealous that while she's trapped at Red Soil Ranch, Lauren gets to spend a free summer in Vermont. Walking back to her bunk, Carly remembers the way Professor Pietro ended his last class and imagines the Lensky family hiking along lush mountain trails singing "Do-Re-Mi" the way the von Trapp family does in *The Sound of Music.* Thinking about the Lenskys makes Carly feel even more homesick than usual, and even though she's used to not getting much mail from her parents, she can't help wishing they would send something.

On Saturday night, Red Soil Ranch has a square dance in the main house with its "brother" camp, a mile away across Moonstone Lake. When Carly arrives, a fat man with a very red face and a string tie is playing the fiddle and calling the dances. The director's wife, wearing a long plaid skirt and a white apron, is serving graham crackers and bug juice punch from a big black stewpot. She scoops exactly half a soup ladle full of the watery orange liquid into Carly's paper cup and reminds her to save the cup in case she wants seconds.

Carly has never square-danced and has no interest in participating. The whole setup seems totally phony compared with scenes she loves watching on *Little House on the Prairie,* where

Pa plays the fiddle and Laura and her sisters dance around the campfire with their friendly neighbor, Isaiah Edwards.

To avoid being asked to join in, Carly slinks off to a dark corner of the room, sips her punch, and watches Rhona gyrating and slinging her hips as she do-si-do's with the head cowboy, a craggy-faced, Western-drawling, bowlegged, balding man named Sonny that all the older girls in camp have fallen in love with. Carly thinks the draw is his clear eyes—blue as the Colorado sky—and the way he looks you up and down when you unsaddle and rub down the horses.

At the end of the evening, the lights dim as the caller puts aside his fiddle and announces that it's time for a last "regular social dance." In his country twang, he pronounces it "regaller." By now he has big sweat stains under the arms of his shirt. As he begins crooning "Blame It on the Rain" into the raspy microphone, a tall, skinny dark-haired boy with a face full of acne comes over and asks Carly to dance.

"I'm Lance," he says, and grabs her low around her waist, pushing her right against him so she feels his rock-hard erection pressing into her. As he grinds his pelvis harder and harder against her tummy and hips, she stares out over his shoulder, trying to look like she's not aware of what's going on down below.

Sometime during the dance, when she feels like she can't bear another moment, the pressure of his body against hers lets up, and she realizes, as she hears him suck in air, that he just came. When the dance finally ends and they separate, the front of his pants are dark and wet. Walking back to her bunk, Carly realizes Lance doesn't even know her name. She stops at the washhouse and goes into one of the foul-smelling stalls. When she puts two fingers down her throat and applies pressure, a thin, orangey liquid and chunks of mealy graham cracker spurt into the toilet.

As disgusting as the evening was for her, Carly decides to use it as fodder for her correspondence with Lauren. Instead of telling what really happened, she plans to embellish her report so Lauren will be impressed by her sexual progress.

Dear Lauren,

Last night at the dance with the boys camp I met this guy named Lance, and we wound up making out behind the barn. He was lying on top of me and wanted to take our clothes off, but I wasn't that much into it. I think he came in his pants. We'll probably get together again next Saturday night, and not because I especially like him but mostly because I'm so bored, I may decide to let him go farther.

Are there any cool dudes in Vermont?

It rained all last week, and one afternoon Rhona from Roslyn taught a bunch of us how to smoke a joint. Mary Ellen doesn't get the difference between smoking pot and just plain smoking and kept calling the joint a cigarette. She sat pouting on her bed, reading the Bible. The rest of us sat in a circle on the floor and passed around the joint. When Mary Ellen said God was gonna punish us, Rhona told her to shut up and keep her repressed religious hang-ups to herself. I think I'll write home to my mom about this so she'll let me come home.

That's the news from Red Soil Reformatory. Write soon and let me know how much better life is on the outside.

Love,

Carly

Carly doesn't mention how sorry she felt for Molly and leaves out the description of how much trouble she had holding the joint. Instead of positioning it between her thumb stump and forefinger, the way everyone else was doing, she alternated hands and lodged the joint between her middle and index fingers, the way movie stars in old movies on television held cigarettes. She stuck her stubby thumbs straight up in the air to keep them out of the way, and while Carly didn't mean to stare, she couldn't help noticing the way the flesh rounded over her stumps and met to form a tiny hole at the tip.

CHAPTER ELEVEN

Carly's doing barn chores when Serena and Jill, who haven't spoken to her since the train trip west, come up and greet her as though they're best buddies.

"Hey, Carly, we've heard the wicked word about your counselor," Serena says.

"Do you guys ever go spy?" Jill asks, raising her eyebrows meaningfully and rolling her eyes toward Serena.

She's wearing one of those Indian beaded belts pulled tightly around her "Yale Sucks" T-shirt.

"What're you talking about?" Carly asks.

Apparently, this is the cue they've been waiting for. They each take one of Carly's arms and lead her off to a clump of tall, blue-green fir trees that shades a clearing behind the barn. Carly learns that her counselor Rhona has been sleeping with Sonny.

"They do it late at night in the ravine that separates the bunks from the main house," Jill tells Carly.

"When you guys are sleeping," Serena continues in a teasing tone of voice.

"So what're we gonna do about it?" Jill is looking straight at Carly as she asks this. "What d'ya think, are you guys game?"

At first Carly thinks she's asking whether she, Mary Ellen, and Molly are willing to sleep with Sonny in the ravine, but then she realizes Jill's talking about something else.

"We're ready to go," Jill is saying. "We've got the Super girls organized for tonight."

Before Carly can make sense of it all, Serena is asking her whether they can count on her to organize the first-year girls. At quarter to midnight, they're all to meet at the flagpole. Everyone should have a flashlight, but no one should use it until they reach the ravine. The older girls think they know the exact spot where Sonny and Rhona "do it" every night, and when they get there—silently so Sonny and Rhona won't realize—the girls will all flash their lights down into the ravine, taking them by complete surprise and catching them in the act.

The raid seems like a crazy idea to Carly, who can't imagine a whole gang of girls being quiet enough to sneak up on Rhona and Sonny without being heard. And once they've shined their flashlights down on them, what are they all supposed to do, just run away?

"I don't know about my bunkmates," Carly starts to protest. "I've got the crippled kid with no big toes, and Mary Ellen's a religious fanatic—"

"Are you making excuses?" Jill cuts her off before she completes her list of reservations. "Are you chicken, or what?"

"It's not me," Carly explains. "It's the others I'm worried about."

"You can convince them, Carly, if you try. We chose you because you're a leader and we believe in you." Serena pats her on the back as she says this.

"We're counting on you, Carly. We know you can do it." Jill squeezes her arm.

Carly mutters that she'll do what she can and turns to leave.

ELIZABETH HARLAN

Behind her she hears one of them say, "You'd better, Carly," and then the other one—Carly can't tell their voices apart—add, "Or else."

Carly gets the same feeling she always gets around the popular kids at school. They're more experienced and know more than she does, as though they have special access to what's going on in the world around them.

On her way back to the bunk, Carly stops by the main house to check her mail cubby. She recognizes her mother's handwriting from the envelope lying with the return address facing up. In spite of herself, Carly's heart lurches, and even though she doesn't like to admit it, she's happy to be hearing from her mom. She tears open the envelope and reads as she walks along the dirt path that leads to the bunk line. Gwen writes about how hot and sticky it is back East and how lucky Carly is to be in the beautiful Rocky Mountains.

Carly realizes Gwen has absolutely zero conception of where Red Soil Ranch is located, miles from any mountains on a parched, waterless flatland where practically the only things that grow are scrub weed and desert cactus. There's no mention of her dad, and at the bottom of the page is a P.S.: *Don't worry. Everyone gets homesick at first. It will pass.* In her next letter, Carly decides, she'll tell Gwen how her counselor spends her nights.

When Carly reaches the rickety footbridge that crosses the ravine, she stands there a while looking down into the ravine in which Rhona and Sonny supposedly "do it" every night. The slopes are lined with rocks and weeds and roots of overturned trees that have long ago dried up and died. Carly can't imagine where a sleeping bag could lie flat in this whole long, rubbly trench.

Molly is sitting on her bed, cutting her toenails, when Carly gets back to the bunk. She has set for herself a nearly impossible task. She holds the scissors between the index and middle finger of her right hand—the same way she holds a joint—and takes forever setting the blades in place, steadying them, and then cutting the toenail. Another thick white curl flies up into the air, and Molly calls out gleefully, "Gotcha!" She follows the trajectory with her beady brown eyes until the nail lands out of sight among the dust balls on the floor. Then she hunkers down over her foot and goes on to the next toe. The fact that she doesn't have big toes doesn't seem to bother her at all or make her the slightest bit self-conscious.

"Where's Mary Ellen?" Carly asks, remembering her assignment from Serena and Jill.

"No idea," Molly says.

"But it's almost dinnertime. Where do you think she could be so late?"

"Dunno."

Carly could kill her for being so useless.

"Guess what I found out?" Carly asks in her most seductive voice.

"Dunno," Molly says again, steadying the scissor blades around what would be a middle toenail if she had big toes.

"You're not gonna believe this, but I had it firsthand from some Super girls—"

"So what? They make up tons of stuff just to impress us."

"But this isn't a lie. It's about Rhona and Sonny and what they do at night together."

Carly watches Molly carefully, hoping for a slight quickening of interest.

"Like what, for instance?" Molly looks up from her toes for the first time.

"Late after we're in bed at night, they meet and do it in the ravine." There's a ring of victory in Carly's voice.

"What? Do what?" Molly asks.

Her face is as blank and impassive as if Carly had told her grass was growing on the ground.

"I don't believe it. I just don't believe what a baby you are, Molly." Carly can't stop the feeling of wanting to be cruel. "Do you mean to tell me you're so dumb and immature you don't understand what 'doing it' means?"

Carly knows she has gone too far, and Molly starts to shout and cry, both at the same time. Carly realizes the moment she begins that Molly's headed for one of her major meltdowns unless she can come up with something fast to distract her.

"Hey, I've got a great idea, Moll, but you have to shut up and listen if you want me to tell you."

Molly sucks up tears and mucus, making a disgusting snorting sound in her nose and throat.

As soon as she calms down, Carly says, "Listen, Moll, if you promise you won't cry anymore, I'll let you be my assistant tonight when we go spy on Rhona and Sonny in the ravine. What d'ya think? Are you game?"

Carly surprises herself at the echo of Serena and Jill's words.

"Maybe. Maybe not. It depends."

Molly's beginning to stage a power play, Carly can tell.

"What does it depend on?"

"You've gotta be nice to me," Molly says, laying aside her nail scissors and sitting up straight and tall. "From now till the end of camp, you have to be my best friend."

"You got it, Moll," Carly says. "I promise."

"That means no more being mean and teasing me, and when other kids act mean, you've gotta make them stop."

"OK, Moll. You've got yourself a deal. Now let me tell you what we're gonna do." Carly likes adopting the big sister role with Molly, which gives her the feeling of having the upper hand.

In the middle of Carly's explanation, Mary Ellen comes in. She's so skinny that her elbows and knees jut out like knobs on her arms and legs. From a distance, in a pair of shorts and a short-sleeve shirt, she looks like a stick figure. Carly decides she'll draw her for her next letter to Lauren.

"Where've you been?" Carly demands, annoyed because she'll have to deal with her next.

"How come you sound so angry, Carly?" Mary Ellen asks. She throws herself down on her bed, as though she's overwhelmed with exhaustion. "I was just up at the main house, reading my mail."

"You won't believe what Carly found out."

Molly sounds more exuberant than Carly has ever heard her, but then Molly checks herself and looks over at Carly, making sure it's OK to go on.

"Can I tell Mary Ellen?" Molly asks.

"Go ahead, Moll," Carly says. "It's OK. Mary Ellen needs to know too."

As Molly explains the situation, Carly realizes Molly has missed some essentials. She understands that Rhona and Sonny meet in the ravine after lights out and that a group of girls is organizing to spy on them tonight, but she obviously doesn't get the part about what they do down there at night.

"Why on earth would anyone want to spy on them?" Mary Ellen asks.

She's screwing up her skinny face in the ugliest way, as though something around her smells like a skunk.

Carly makes an instantaneous decision. She knows Mary Ellen will be scandalized if she hears what Rhona and Sonny are up to. Who knows how she'll react if she actually realizes the sinful stuff that's taking place in her very midst? All sorts of her visions could come up, and then none of them would get a good night's sleep for the rest of the summer. She probably won't go with them to the ravine anyway, so Carly figures it's just as well she knows as little as possible.

"Men aren't supposed to cross the ravine," she tells Mary Ellen officially.

"That's why they call where we live 'No Man's Land,'" Molly pipes up in an unusual display of cleverness, and looks over at Carly for approval.

Carly winks at her and nods enthusiastically.

"Exactly right, Moll. Sonny and Rhona are going against regulations," Carly adds, knowing Mary Ellen, who's very rule oriented, will find this in and of itself objectionable.

"Don't you think we could just say something to Rhona about it," Mary Ellen proposes, "instead of trying to get her in trouble?"

Carly rushes in to stop this drift. "I wouldn't do that. I mean, if we say something to her, she might turn around and get us in trouble with the director."

"Like for doing what?" Molly asks indignantly. "What could she say about us?"

"I don't know," Carly says, thinking hard. "Maybe she'd rat us out for smoking pot. She could deny that she taught us and say that we did it on our own."

"You shouldn't smoke anyway." Mary Ellen is using her prissiest tone of voice. "It's bad for your lungs."

"Let's just go spy on them tonight," Molly coaxes. "It'll be dark, and they won't even know who's doing it to them."

"Well," Mary Ellen says huffily, "if you guys wanna do a jerky, low-down thing like that, you go right ahead and count me out!"

The other first-year girls are a cinch by comparison. They all fall instantly for the intrigue and excitement of the plan and mobilize each other so effectively that by dinnertime Carly's work is done.

The ravine raid is a real bust. At nine, as usual, Rhona grabs her sleeping bag from underneath her bed and leaves the bunk.

"You guys better be good," she warns the way she always does. "Or else I'll personally see to having you murdered in the morning."

As soon as she's gone, Mary Ellen gets down on her hands and knees, makes her little tent with her fingers, recites her prayers, and climbs into bed. The last thing she says before falling asleep is, "God's gonna punish you guys. Just you wait and see."

At ten thirty the sky opens, and a downpour begins, which lasts for the next hour. Carly lies in bed worrying what to do, unsure if the raid is still on or if because of the weather the Super girls have called it off. Molly keeps asking every ten minutes or so, "Is it time yet, Carly?"

Carly tells her to shut up and lie still. When the time comes, she'll let her know.

At eleven forty Carly decides to go over to Serena and Jill's bunk to see what's going on. She tells Molly she's checking things out and will come right back to get her. She goes off alone in the dark toward the Super bunks. Serena and Jill are tucked tightly away in their beds when Carly gets there.

She whispers to them, "Hey, what's up?" and they grunt back at her that it's off for tonight.

"Tomorrow night, if it's clear," Jill moans sleepily.

"Go back to bed," Serena sneers as Carly leaves their bunk.

When she gets back, Mary Ellen is still sleeping soundly, but there's no trace of Molly. Carly pulls her covers away to check if she's underneath them, but her bed is empty. Carly walks outside and circles the bunk a couple times, but Molly's nowhere around. It occurs to her that maybe Molly thought she had taken off for the ravine without her and went out to follow. Carly checks the shelf by the door, and sure enough, Molly has taken her flashlight.

Just as Carly's deciding how to handle this disaster, she hears people approaching on the path outside the bunk. As they come closer, Molly's crying, muffled at first, gets louder and louder.

"Who the hell do you think you are coming out after me like that?"

Carly recognizes Rhona's voice from the dentalized *d*'s and the dropped *r*'s of her Long Island accent. As Molly comes into view, Carly sees that her pajamas are covered with mud. Even her face is wet and smeared.

"My hands hurt," she's sobbing, "and my feet and face and all of me from falling in the ravine."

"Oh my God, Molly," Carly gasps, "what a mess you are!"

"You get the hell in bed," Rhona screams at her, "and don't you dare move a muscle until morning!"

Rhona's shirt is unbuttoned all the way down the front, and she doesn't have a bra underneath. She gives Molly a shove that sends her reeling across the floor. For the rest of the night, Carly hears Molly whimpering in her bed. Her breath catches every now and then, and Carly worries that before morning comes, she'll stop breathing and be dead.

The next day's not a shower day, but Carly washes Molly down and gives her a shampoo, using the garden hose behind the barn. Molly's sitting on her bed, painting her toenails with bright purple polish, when the director's wife comes through the door of their bunk. She doesn't knock or say, "Hello in there." It's the first time Carly has seen her in jeans and a sweatshirt. Realization dawns: what a fraud she is in her down-home, long plaid skirt with the white apron she wears at dances.

"I'd like to speak to you privately," the director's wife tells Molly. "Come with me right away."

"But my nails are wet," Molly whines, and applies another coat to her pinky toenail. The polish is frosted, and Molly's toes shimmer as she wiggles them dry.

"Never mind, Molly, come right now."

Carly watches Molly out the screen window of the bunk, hobbling along barefooted behind the director's wife. She doesn't realize it's the last time she'll be seeing her. They learn at dinner that Molly is staying at the main house until the morning, when she'll be sent home by plane to Cleveland. The word of her getting kicked out spreads from table to table and from one camper to the next until the entire dining room is humming with the news. While everyone around her acts like getting expelled from camp is the worst thing that could happen, Carly is jealous that Molly's going home.

Plus, even though Carly never really liked her as a friend, and even though Molly often got on her nerves, Carly feels guilty for letting her down and not doing a better job of looking after her. If Molly really had been her younger sister, that would mean Carly wasn't a very good big sister after all.

When they get back to the bunk, all of Molly's clothes and personal stuff have been cleared away. The only trace left is the bottle of purple polish, which has tipped over and dried in an iridescent puddle on the floor.

CHAPTER
TWELVE

Dear Lauren,

Lance stole a sleeping bag from the hike house at the boys camp and brings it when we meet at night in a ravine here at Red Soil Ranch. He also brings condoms, and we've gotten nude together and gone to third base but not all the way yet. I'm still making up my mind about whether I like him enough to lose my virginity with him. I know you didn't care about that with Elliott, but I'd like feeling at least a little bit in love with someone I'm going to let go all the way with me.

Camp still sucks. I'll keep you posted on all developments. And write me a real letter one of these days instead of just sending postcards with cows!

Love, Carly

In her letter to her parents, Carly piles on as many complaints about Red Soil Ranch as she can fit on the front and back side of the page of camp stationery that's handed out every Sunday for writing letters home.

She avoids saying she's homesick because she knows Gwen

will use that as her reason for not letting her come home. "It will pass," she already wrote back once, so instead Carly closes with the clincher:

> *This camp is the worst supervised place I've ever been. At night our counselor sleeps in the ravine with the head cowboy, and on rainy days she teaches us how to smoke pot.*
> *Love, Carly*

Carly would give anything to laze around in bed when she's awakened on Sunday morning by the bugle blaring reveille, but campers have to turn up at breakfast in the main house by seven thirty, and a required hike up a local mountain called Haystack is on today's schedule.

Carly knows she has to figure out some way to make the time go by. Better yet, to make this whole horrible camp scene go away. She has always felt out of place, like an outsider, but this summer she feels it more painfully than ever. She wonders if her mother knew how truly depressed she has become, she'd relent and let her come home. As a psychiatrist, Carly figures, she should recognize signs of danger when a patient is getting worse and worse.

The mornings are cold at Red Soil Ranch even though it's summer, so Carly puts on long pants and a sweatshirt before heading to the washhouse. The water's never really hot, so Carly brushes her teeth but skips splashing water on her face. She has neither the interest nor the energy to brush the tangles out of her hair, which she stuffs into a tieback before heading off to breakfast.

Clouds of dust form as Carly kicks up the dry turf with the point of her boot on her way to the main house, and an idea begins to take shape. What if she really did take a turn for the worse? What if she got sick or somehow couldn't function the way she knows her parents are expecting her to do? She's just supposed to put up with all of this: with these awful kids she doesn't know and doesn't care about, with the dirty, smelly bunk with the lumpy, thin mattress and the scratchy sheets, the once-a-week shower that comes out in a cold trickle that makes it impossible to really get clean, with her counselor who could care less about her and her bunkmates. Why should she play by the rules when her parents have broken the rules of taking care of their own kid?

Carly wonders if Molly had some of these feelings of how unfair it was to be sent to this horrible place. It takes Carly totally by surprise, but she misses Molly. It's like the homesick feeling she always has, even knowing how bad it often feels to be home.

An hour later, when the camp bus lets them off at the base of Haystack, Carly hangs back as the rest of the group begins to file along the trail. The sun is high in the sky and heating up, and Carly's sorry she's wearing long sleeves and long pants. Other kids were smart enough to put on shorts and tank tops, and Carly's already feeling hot and sweaty. On a sudden impulse, when everyone is in front of her, facing up the trail, Carly darts off onto an alternative trail with a sign marked "Clifford Falls." The idea of cool, rushing water is much more appealing than hiking up a mountain.

In just a few paces, Carly is deep within the woods. She can still hear voices of campers on the trail that forked away toward Haystack, but she can't see them any longer through the leafy trees and thicket of shrubs, and no one can see her either. Carly's panicked someone will come after her and discover that she has broken ranks with the camp group. It feels like committing some horrible crime, and Carly battles with herself about whether she should head back and catch up with the others. But after a few more minutes, she hears the sound of falling water in the distance and is propelled by the thought of getting to fresh water.

At the sight of the falls cascading into a frothing pool lined with large boulders, Carly strips down to her bra and panties, hesitates and looks around to make sure she's alone, and then gets totally nude. She dips her toes in the icy water, splashes water on her face, sits down on a boulder, and slowly lowers herself into the pool. The water is ice-cold, but the sun overhead is hot, and Carly knows she'll warm up fast once she comes out. It feels amazing to immerse herself fully in the clear, cold water, to dunk her head and rinse her hair, over and over again, to run her hands over her body, in her armpits and between her thighs and buttocks, in her private parts that haven't felt clean since she took the long train trip to Red Soil Ranch.

Nothing has felt this good since she has been away, and being clean again absolves Carly of the sense of wrongdoing. How can it be bad to seek out fresh water and cleanse herself? Aren't people supposed to look after themselves, and if they're deprived of something they need, isn't it good to seek it out? She thinks of Laura in *Little House on the Prairie*. If she were hot and sweaty and dirty all over and she was on a hike and came upon fresh water, Carly's sure she'd do the same.

After her swim, Carly lies on a slab of rock. Her body absorbs the heat of the stone from below and of the sun from above. Red and black dots float behind her closed eyes, and she gets drowsy and falls asleep.

A fly buzzing incessantly around her head awakens her. Carly comes to with a start and doesn't remember where she is. When she does, she panics and grabs her clothes, dresses as fast as she can, and starts back over the same path she took before.

She has no idea how long she slept or how long she has been separated from the others. She doesn't know what time they were due back at the bus from the hike up Haystack, and even if she knew, without a watch she has no way of knowing if she's early or late.

The closer she gets to the trailhead, the more worried she becomes about what she'll say to explain her absence. Maybe she can just blend back into the group, but the chances are, she realizes, someone will have noticed she was missing or that she came back from another direction.

But for all of what she worries about, what happens when she returns is beyond her worst imaginings. As she comes out into the clearing where she split off from the camp group, Carly sees a police car with a bright red flashing light. Two policemen are standing outside the car, talking to one of the counselors and taking notes on a pad of paper. A girl named Jenny sees Carly first, points her arm at her and screams her name so loud that everyone turns to look at her as she emerges from the woods. A few kids break out in applause, but as soon as the policemen start approaching Carly, the crowd falls silent.

Carly feels suddenly faint. If she doesn't sit down and put her head between her knees, she's afraid she's going to pass out. But before she can do anything, the policemen and the counselor surround her and start questioning her about where she has been.

"I got lost," Carly stammers. "I took the wrong trail."

"And where did you go?" one of the officers asks her. "It has been several hours since you were separated from the camp group."

"I tried to find my way back to the trail to Haystack but wound up at Clifford Falls."

"And had a nice little swim while you were there?" the counselor interjects.

Carly reaches for her hair and realizes it's still wet.

Someone calls out, "Yeah, right. I would've liked a cool swim instead of a sweltering hike up Haystack!" and the rest of the campers break out in laughter.

The officers and the counselor start talking among themselves, and Carly picks up only bits and pieces of their conversation—". . . hasn't come to harm," "case closed," "camp disciplinary matter"—before the counselor takes her firmly by the arm.

"Get on the bus and sit in the front seat behind the driver," he tells her. "The director will deal with you when we return to camp."

Carly gets the same worried feeling she got at school when she was sent to Ms. Harrington's office, but this feels bigger and scarier, as though this time she has really gone too far and broken something much worse than just a rule.

The director is a tall, strict-looking man with white hair and a deep suntan. Carly has seen him only once before, at a dinner in the main house when he came to welcome the campers and tell them how much fun they were in for at Red Soil Ranch. He spreads his hands wide on his desk and looks up over his half glasses as he speaks in a scary deep voice.

"What you did when you went missing is very serious, young lady. You not only upset an entire camp expedition, you caused us to reach out to local authorities, who in turn sent out patrols to scour the mountainside. It's unthinkable that you decided to split off from the group in order to indulge in a swim, with no thought that people would worry that you had come to harm."

Carly doesn't know how to respond and just keeps nodding her head up and down to demonstrate that she understands how serious this matter is.

"We have no choice but to send you home, because the

example you set of utter disregard for the camp community and its rules cannot be sanctioned here at Red Soil Ranch. We'll be calling your parents, and arrangements will be made."

When Carly says nothing, the director clears his throat and raises his voice. "There's nothing to smile about. This is not a trivial matter, young lady."

Carly hadn't realized she was smiling and changes her expression. "No, sir."

She wonders how her parents will react when they get the call. She imagines them being scared that something awful happened to her. She'll have to explain a million things to them about what she did and why, and what she was thinking or not thinking. She knows they'll be upset and angry, but none of that matters. Carly's feeling much better, and the scared, uncertain feeling she has been living with ever since coming back from Clifford Falls and seeing the police car is turning into vast relief.

The director's telling her that she needs to pack up her things and report to the main house, where she'll be staying until her departure, but Carly's barely listening. What's happening doesn't feel like punishment at all. It's a miracle that she's finally getting her way and going home. Maybe Molly felt the same way. Carly imagines her in her home in a Cleveland suburb, cuddled in her mother's lap.

As Carly packs her clothes, Rhona shows up at the bunk and tells her she's scheduled to leave early in the morning.

"The camp van will take you to the airport. When you get to LaGuardia, look for a driver holding a sign with your name on it."

Rhona bangs the screen door closed as she leaves.

"I'll keep you in my prayers," Mary Ellen says.

"It's not like I'm dying," Carly retorts. "I'm the lucky one who's getting out of this hellhole."

CHAPTER
THIRTEEN

With the two-hour time difference between Mountain and Eastern time, and after changing planes in Chicago, it's already dark when Carly reaches LaGuardia. The driver holding a sign with her name is waiting for her by baggage claim.

When she arrives at the apartment, her parents call her into the living room. Gwen sits on one end of the sofa, and Joel sits on the other. Carly takes the seat across from them, as though she's having an interview, in the taupe tweed chair with the buttons with matching fabric sewn on the seat.

"We want to hear about what happened at camp, Carly," her mother begins, "but we have something else very important to discuss with you."

It's late July, and the temperature outside is close to a hundred. Inside, the window air conditioner is straining at full capacity. It makes a low, humming sound that every now and then grows louder.

"Your father and I have been struggling with some serious problems of our own, Carly, and we've agreed that it would be best for us and for the family if we were to separate."

Carly's breathing grows more labored and merges with the

heaving of the air conditioner, making her afraid that at any moment it might explode. There's so much wrong with what she has just heard that she doesn't know where to begin organizing her thoughts, much less a response. "Best for the family"? Carly doesn't think so. "*If* we were to separate"? Carly knows already that this is a foregone conclusion. Isn't that why she was sent away? Isn't that why it really doesn't matter what happened to her at camp, because her being away allowed this to happen? She should have fought harder, Carly realizes. She should have stayed home and never left for camp. Now she knows she has been merely a pawn in a game in which her parents were the only players that mattered.

Joel leaves soon afterwards. He kisses Carly goodbye and leaves her and Gwen alone. Gwen asks a few questions about camp, but Carly's not in the mood to talk. She was planning to tell her parents about how awful her time at Red Soil Ranch was, how badly run the place is, and how unfair it was to kick her out because she got lost on a trail, but all that's behind her now. Her parents, whose lives have changed so absolutely, were keeping secrets from her.

The first thing she does when she's alone in her room is call Lauren.

"I got kicked out. It's a long story."

"Hey, at least the internment is over. Tell me all about what forms of torture they used."

"I just found out my parents are getting divorced."

There's a long pause when Lauren doesn't say anything, and Carly thinks maybe it isn't such a great idea that she called her.

"That sucks," Lauren finally whispers. "That's some homecoming they arranged for you."

Carly doesn't know what to say, and at the same time she realizes that there's nothing to say. No words would make any difference at all.

Lauren continues, "I didn't realize they were having problems. Did you have any idea?"

"I never really thought about it," Carly tells her.

"Are you gonna be OK?"

"Yeah, it's fine. I don't really care one way or the other. My
father was never around anyway. What's going on with you?"

"The usual. Nothing much. Oh, by the way, Tibou's having
a baby."

"Wow. When?"

"Some time around New Year's."

"You never told me she was pregnant." Carly welcomes the
chance to change the subject.

"She just started showing and telling people over the
summer."

"You're not exactly 'people.'" It's easier, Carly discovers, to
commiserate with Lauren than to have to respond to Lauren's
concern for her.

When Lauren doesn't say anything else, Carly announces,
"I'd better get started unpacking. Speak to you soon?"

"Right. Hey, Carly, I'm sorry about everything that's going
on."

"At least they didn't beat up on me for getting kicked out of
camp."

"Well, now that you're back with nothing to do, how about
you come up to Vermont and hang out for a while?" Lauren asks.

"I'd like that."

"Great."

"I'll call you soon."

That night Carly dreams she's a furry gray squirrel, a real-life version of the stuffed squirrel she has slept with every night since
she was little. In the dream she's racing toward the top of an

enormous oak tree. Just as she's about to get there, way up near the sky where the branches thin and bend under her weight, she loses her footing and falls recklessly groundward. She never actually crashes, because the dream ends and Carly wakes, breathless and panicky as though she's actually about to die.

Carly switches on the light and throws her feet over the side of the bed. The clock on the night table glows its yellow-green digital message that it's four thirty, but Carly doesn't want to go back to sleep in case the nightmare repeats itself, which often happens when she dreams scary stuff.

Instead, she goes over to her desk, tilts back on her chair, and begins to think about how her mother and father would feel if something happened to her and she were going to die. Her parents have made it clear for so long—forever as far as Carly can remember—that they expect her future to include a solid and well-defined career, like being a teacher or a lawyer.

At various stages they've pushed all the obvious traditional options at her. Physics when she showed a vague aptitude for math in sixth grade. Architecture when she got an A- in Mr. Kessler's drafting class in junior high school. Medicine when she showed interest in dissecting a pregnant mouse in biology last year. Joel even cut out an article from a flight magazine about the United States Space Camp in Huntsville, Alabama, where kids from all over the country go to play astronaut for a week. But none of her parents' ideas ever feel like something that Carly could actually imagine herself being or doing.

It's hard to imagine how her parents would react if she died and what they would do if they could not be anxious about Carly's future. Maybe they'd just relax, Carly thinks, after getting over the big hump of their initial grief. Her dad has moved out anyway. Her mom could use Carly's bedroom to store the files that are beginning to overflow from her office. The more convinced Carly becomes that her absence wouldn't really matter, the sadder and more depressed she becomes.

Carly decides to change the subject and dredges up a memory of how much she liked dissecting that mouse last year. The process made her think about what it would feel like to grow a baby of her own. Having a big family doesn't seem like a bad idea, actually, when she thinks of it. A batch of kids could be a lot of fun. Having an only child is definitely not part of the picture she visualizes for herself. Parents being disappointed if you don't turn out just the way they want you to. No way Carly would do that to a kid of her own.

If you have lots of kids, she figures, you won't care too much about any one of them, and even if you do, if one doesn't turn out the way you hope, there's always another one to make up for it. She wonders how many more babies Tibou's planning to have.

Carly pictures herself wearing blue jeans, a T-shirt, and a calico apron, with her bushy red hair tied in a pigtail. She sees herself flipping pancakes over a big metal skillet in a kitchen with pineapples stenciled on the wallpaper. Some of the pancakes flip onto the floor, and no one gets upset. Carly believes it's important for mothers to be young and cool and not to lose touch with their kids, so she plans to do lots of activities with them like playing ball and building sandcastles on the beach and watching the same TV shows they watch.

A vague worry is gnawing at Carly about the connection between her parents getting divorced and her being an only child. She knows they've always wished she was different from the way she is, and she wonders if they'd had another kid, one who turned out better, maybe they'd have been happier and stayed together.

CHAPTER FOURTEEN

I t's well past noon when Carly, still in her pajamas, comes down to the kitchen.

"Morning," Carly says to her mother's back.

Gwen turns around and mouths, "Want one?" She points at the sandwich she's fixing while talking on the phone. "That meeting was rescheduled for next week, Sam. No, the report is still due by Friday."

Carly opens the refrigerator, surveys its contents, and takes out a container of orange juice.

"The tests will be done by the end of today." Gwen continues talking into the phone as she spreads tuna fish salad on a slice of bread. "And then we'll have some information to work with."

When Carly starts drinking directly from the container, Gwen scowls at her and mimes pouring into a glass. Carly goes to the cupboard and takes one out.

"Right. Let's talk later, when the test results come through. Thanks, Sam."

Gwen hangs up the phone and turns to Carly.

"Would you like a sandwich? I was just making myself one for lunch."

"I'm kind of on a breakfast schedule."

"At one in the afternoon?"

"It's only twelve thirty, and I was tired."

"It's true you had a long day of travel yesterday," Gwen says. "How do you feel?"

"You mean, after getting kicked out of camp and traveling and changing planes for a whole day and coming home to find out you and Dad are getting divorced? I feel great."

Gwen's face shows the angry and impatient look that she has whenever Carly's uncooperative. "Sarcasm isn't going to help you feel better."

"It's not like you and Dad gave me a heads-up or anything. I come home after being sent away to some shithole summer camp to find out you've busted up our family behind my back."

Gwen's expression softens, and her voice quavers with uncertainty. "It's complicated, Carly, and I know we didn't prepare you for what you came home to, but we weren't prepared for your coming home so soon. We were still working out a plan."

"Like it would've been different if I'd come home on time?"

"Well, we were thinking that one of us might have gone out to meet you and to bring you home."

"How thoughtful of you. I wish you had. Then you would've seen what a dump the place was."

"I realize it didn't meet your expectations, Carly."

"I wasn't the one who had expectations. That would be you, who chose the place."

Carly pours juice from the container into the glass, drinks it down, and fills it again.

Gwen slices her sandwich and holds up the two halves. "You sure you don't want to share this, at least?"

"No thanks. I'm good with juice."

"Which you shouldn't drink from the container, Carly."

"I got that," Carly says, holding up the full glass as though she's toasting her mother. Some of the juice spills on the floor, which Carly swipes with her bare foot.

Gwen takes a paper napkin and wipes up the smear. "Well, I'm sorry the camp didn't work out, Carly, and now that you're home, let's talk about structuring the rest of your summer."

"Lauren invited me to Vermont. Can I go? By the way, Tibou's pregnant."

"What? Mrs. Lensky's in her forties!"

"Well, she's having a baby anyway."

"My goodness. Do you know when she's due?"

"Sometime around New Year's."

"The Lenskys certainly have a lot on their plate—with their move to California and now a new baby coming."

"Can I go visit Lauren in Vermont?" Carly asks again.

"Yes, that would be fine, Carly, but I think it's best to first line up a plan for the rest of your time before school starts in the fall. Once you have a plan, then we can work out a visit to Vermont."

"What kind of plan? It's not like there are all sorts of programs around for kids who get kicked out of camp."

"Maybe you could volunteer at the hospital. I know the supervisor of the children's floor, Susan Jamieson, is always looking for extra hands to help out with activities for the kids."

"You mean, kids who are sick?"

"Well, the ones who are well enough to play while they're getting better and waiting to be released."

"Or waiting to die?"

"Carly!" Gwen chides. "What a thing to say."

"They don't all get well."

"That's true, but they all need to feel they have something to live for. Play is an important part of getting better. Shall I give Susan a call? The work could count toward your community service requirement at school this year."

"I'll think about it."

"Sleeping till noon everyday isn't an option, young lady."

"I just got home, for Chrissake!"

"I realize that, Carly, and now that you're home, you need to make a plan."

"Yeah right, and who made the plan for Dad running off with his swooshy assistant Edwin?"

Carly knows she caught her mom off guard when she sees her go still and silent. Her eyes open so wide and stare so hard that Carly looks away.

"They didn't see me, but I saw them holding hands in a restaurant."

"That must have been shocking. I'm so sorry it happened that way. I've been wanting your father to discuss this with you, Carly. I felt he should be the one to bring it up."

"You mean, you didn't want to rat him out about busting up your marriage 'cause he's gay?"

"I felt it was for him to share this with you."

"Like he's really gonna tell me about how he and his boy-friend are getting it on."

"We don't always get to choose who we are, Carly."

"But we get to choose who we marry, right, and then to fuck it up because of who we are?"

Gwen looks so sad and defeated that Carly suddenly feels sorry for her. "I guess I could give Ms. Jamieson a call."

Gwen's voice sounds far less insistent than before when she says, "Yes, maybe so. I'll go find her number for you," before leaving the room.

CHAPTER FIFTEEN

Voices of kids playing in the meadow carry across Fifth Avenue as Carly walks north from Ninety-Sixth Street. She drags slowly on her cigarette, trying to make it last, because they don't allow smoking at Mount Sinai Hospital, where she's heading for her interview with Susan Jamieson to help out with activities for sick children who feel well enough to do something other than lie in bed and sleep.

Over the top of the stone wall that lines Central Park, separating it from the street, Carly can see heads bob up and down and flashes of bright-colored clothing worn by happy, healthy kids who haven't been kicked out of camp and aren't sick and dying—lucky kids who get to spend their summer days running around and playing in the park.

Carly can't shuck the feeling of guilt about getting angry at her mother about Joel and Edwin. It's not her mom's fault that she married the wrong person and that now she's left with the mess this mistake has made of all of their lives. There's nothing much Carly can do to make any of this go away, and even though she's not particularly excited about doing volunteer work at Mount Sinai Hospital, she hopes the interview will go well and that her mom will be pleased if Carly gets the job.

Susan Jamieson has short, cropped hair and big hoop earrings, and seems very young and friendly. She dresses kind of casual: a shirt that isn't tucked in over jeans and sneakers with no socks.

While Ms. Jamieson talks to Carly in her office, she watches everything that's going on in the playroom from behind a big glass window. "Oh God, that's Richard," she gasps as a stretcher covered with a sheet is wheeled by. The other kids look thunderstruck as they peek around from what they're doing at the play tables. A little girl with a bandage around her head begins to cry.

"This is what happens when a child needs to be taken off the floor," Ms. Jamieson explains in a quiet, serious voice that makes Carly realize what she's really saying is that this is what happens when a child dies.

Ms. Jamieson stands up abruptly and leaves the office. Once on the playroom floor, she starts clapping her hands and calling for volunteers for a muffin-baking project. The kids all raise their hands and call, "Me, me, me," as she whips out spoons and bowls and bags of flour and sugar.

"Grab one of those blue coats from a peg by my door," she calls back to Carly, "and come lend a hand."

As the muffins bake in the oven, Carly helps a little Black girl named Germaine write a letter to her grandmother. Instead of writing out all the words, Germaine draws pictures of the things like "bed" and "doctor." She asks for Carly's help to draw the intravenous contraption that rolls around the floor and goes everywhere with her, even to the bathroom.

"How do you spell 'tomorrow'?" Germaine asks, tugging on the sleeve of Carly's blue smock. "I'm getting over leukemia," she explains, "and going home."

Carly slowly spells out "tomorrow," and watches as Germaine writes the rest of the sentence: *Tomorrow I be home.*

Carly isn't sure this is true, but she gets the feeling it's OK for the kids to write whatever they want. It's amazing how Germaine doesn't mind one bit that she's bald as a bat. Carly thinks she'd personally rather be dead than go around with no hair. For sure, she decides, if she ever goes bald, she'll get a big, gorgeous wig. Something like her mother's patient Annelies's hair, lots of thick dark curls that fly wild and float in the air as she moves.

Under the word "love" at the bottom of the letter, Germaine draws a picture and labels it "ME." She makes a head with a whole bunch of braids sticking up all around. It comes out looking like a smiling sun sending out rays of light.

The morning passes so quickly that Carly's surprised when Ms. Jamieson comes over to let her know it's past noon and time to go home.

"How much free time do you have, Carly?" she asks. "I've got a regular afternoon volunteer this summer, but I could use your help five mornings a week, if you can manage that."

"Sure. I can do that," Carly says. "Thanks, Ms. Jamieson."

"Thank *you*, Carly. See you tomorrow at nine, then. And by the way, you handled a hard one very well today, when Richard died and was taken away."

"What'd he die of?" Carly asks.

"He had a brain tumor," Ms. Jamieson says quietly, placing a hand on Carly's shoulder. "The kind that didn't get better."

Carly nods, trying to take this in. "Did he know he was dying?"

"I don't think so. I don't think any of us know for sure what distinguishes the miracle of life from death."

Ms. Jamieson goes on to explain the way they handle things on the children's floor. You're not supposed to talk to the kids about what's the matter with them, but if they bring it up, it's OK to listen. You can even say something sensitive and sympathetic, as long as you keep it cheery. You're never supposed to react like you think the kid might actually not be getting better.

"And here, you can put this name tag on your coat, Carly, and leave it on a peg in my office. Oh, and call me Susan. Everyone else does."

Just before leaving the hospital, Carly is seized by a sudden impulse. She stops by the administrative office and asks the grayhaired lady behind the window if there are special forms people can fill out to donate organs. The lady lowers her half glasses onto the tip of her nose and looks Carly up and down, as much of her as she can see over the counter and out the slit of window, and asks, "Surely not for you?"

"Oh no, of course not. It's for a report I have to make for school. You know, for my community service requirement."

"Well, in that case . . ."

The woman replaces her glasses on the bridge of her nose and hands Carly a set of papers fastened with a paper clip.

"Of course, they must be notarized to be made official," the woman tells her, "and signed by a parent in the case of a minor."

On her way out of the hospital, Carly passes a large auditorium. The back doors are open onto the hall, and Carly hears the familiar voice of a woman speaking at the far end of the room. She stops and looks inside. She watches, astonished, as her mother talks before a room filled with people.

"Every parent breathes a wish into the child. The wish may be a secret—unseen by both parent and child—but like an invisible light that illuminates a space even when we cannot see its source, so the wish illuminates and gives breath to the life of the child."

When Gwen looks up and smiles at the audience, Carly

jumps back behind the doorframe, afraid she might be seen. Gwen takes a sip of water and begins reading again:

"It's the adolescent's task to uncover the secret forces that have over-determined his or her life up to this point. Once the parental wish is laid bare—embraced, resisted, or rejected as necessary—the adolescent begins the job, which lasts throughout adult life, of shaping and forming her self-chosen destiny."

To Carly, Gwen looks very formal, almost like a talking statue in her navy-blue suit with the white silk blouse. From Carly's surprised perspective—she had no idea her mother would be speaking here today—the words coming out of Gwen's mouth, the gestures of her hands, and the movements of her head are strangely disjointed. It's as though Carly knows who's speaking, hears what's being said, but somehow can't connect these impressions with her mother. Nothing Gwen has said, not one single word about kids and how they grow and how parents are supposed to see who they are and help them become themselves, connects with anything Carly has ever felt happening in her own relationship with her mother.

At the first crack of applause, Gwen removes her eyeglasses and begins collecting her papers. A tall, thin man with a bright pink bow tie is clapping as he crosses the stage. He extends his arm as though he's about to shake hands with Gwen, but when he reaches her, they hug instead. Could this be her mom's new boyfriend? Carly wonders as she dashes away.

That evening, as Carly gets ready for bed, she finds herself actually looking forward to returning to the hospital in the morning. She imagines herself coming onto the floor and having a kid who remembers her run up and greet her with a smiling face. She especially likes the blue volunteer smock she gets to wear—a little like the crisp, official doctors' coats—which is big and loose and hides her safely inside.

It's not that Carly wants to get sick and die, but she can't help feeling envious of all the fuss that's made over the kids in the hospital. Take the playroom, for example, filled with paint and clay and video machines and a pool table and air hockey and baskets of candy and snacks that the staff leaves around.

Carly's mind drifts into a make-believe scenario in which Susan Jamieson is her mother. She imagines them living all alone—in the fantasy Susan doesn't have a husband—and making puzzles and playing Scrabble and Trivial Pursuit and maybe even sewing clothes together like old-fashioned mothers and daughters used to do, as in *Little House on the Prairie*.

Carly's only experience of being in a hospital, other than when she was born, which doesn't count since she can't remember it, was when she was twelve years old and had emergency surgery for a false-alarm appendectomy. The attack came on slowly, beginning when Carly was playing at her friend Joan Ellen Johnson's house on a Friday after school, and getting worse through the weekend and the following week, which Carly spent at home sick. In the end, the pain in her side had become so severe that her pediatrician, Dr. Miner, was forced to reconsider her earlier diagnosis of stomach flu and advised Gwen and Joel to have Carly hospitalized for tests.

Carly remembers her parents sitting on either side of her cranked-up hospital bed in a room she shared with a girl named Michaela, who had a tumor in her leg removed the day before. Michaela awakened every hour or so to vomit from the aftereffects of anesthesia and then to go back to sleep. Her mother, who never left her side, held a triangular metal pan under Michaela's chin and mopped her forehead with a damp washcloth. Carly never got to talk with Michaela, because within the first day of testing it was decided that Carly needed immediate surgery.

Gwen, who sat on Carly's right side, did the explaining. The team of doctors who examined Carly suspected appendicitis. The only way to know for sure, and to stay on the safe side, was to operate.

"Sometimes that's what it is, and then they remove the appendix," Gwen explained. "And sometimes it's just a very bad stomachache caused by something else, and it just passes."

Joel said nothing until Gwen finished her explanations and the orderly who was standing by transferred Carly to the rolling stretcher that would whisk her away to the operating room.

"Whatever it is," Joel told her, cupping his large hand over her pale limp one to which the IV was connected by a plastic, arrow-shaped tube, "they're going to make it all better."

Carly remembers the expression of love and concern on her father's face when he said this and her feeling, at the time, that he was the most powerful person in the world. He doesn't seem anything like that anymore, and she can't remember a time in recent history when her father didn't seem nervous and preoccupied with himself. He didn't even remember her sixteenth birthday last spring. Now, as she thinks back, she wonders if, when she was in the hospital, her father had already started seeing Edwin.

When Carly awakened, she was in the same hospital room as before, only it was filled with flowers and balloons. Michaela's bed was made up fresh, and she was gone. That evening the surgeon came to talk to Carly's parents. He came right after her dinner tray had been delivered: slices of chicken, a ball-shaped scoop of mashed potatoes, a mound of green peas with little dents in the sides, and a cube of red gelatin that jiggled as the nurse rolled the tray table across the bed. The surgeon, wearing pale blue pajamas, never looked at Carly once. She wondered if he wore a matching pale blue cap because he was bald.

He shifted his weight from one leg to the other while at the same time switching hands on his hips. Whichever hand was free, he held it out toward her parents, his fingers spread wide and curled inward toward each other, carving the air as though it were a lump of moist clay. He explained that in fact Carly had not had appendicitis. When they opened her up, they found nothing wrong with her appendix and nothing to explain the pain. Gwen and Joel kept nodding as though they approved.

When the surgeon left, her parents stayed with Carly and tried to make her eat the food that sat cold and untouched on her tray. At ten o'clock an announcement was made on a loudspeaker that visiting hours were over. Carly was far too nauseated to eat. She managed a sip or two of water before her parents left for the night.

The next morning when Gwen and Joel came to visit, they brought Carly things from home: one of her own flannel nighties printed with pink and yellow flowers, a hardcover, illustrated copy of *Heidi* that Carly was given at Christmas by her aunt Julia and that Gwen had been prodding her to read, and a stack of magazines. The book weighed too painfully on Carly's stitches when she tried to read it, and her eyes refused to focus on the tiny print.

Instead, she read an article in the latest copy of *Discover* magazine, which had a picture on the cover of magnified cells that looked like squiggly marbles all in the same blotchy, grayish color. The picture went with a story that told about how cancer is formed. Sometimes, the article explained, a good cell runs away and turns bad—like kids who run away from home and get into trouble—and then the bad cell starts to gang up on the other good cells and turn them into more bad cells. The bad cells hang out together until they make a big lump called a tumor. Carly thought of her cat Sticky Buns, who got one of them in her side a couple years ago and had to be put to sleep.

For the first few days after the surgery Carly didn't notice the stomach pain anymore, just the pain from the incision. But when she got home from the hospital and the incision wound began to heal, the other pain returned. Only this time Carly didn't mention it to Gwen and Joel. She'd already figured out an explanation for the events of the past couple weeks. Carly assumed she was really much sicker than anyone was admitting. In fact, she was convinced she had incurable cancer. She had heard of such cases, in which surgeons cut people open and then close them up because the cancer is buried too deep inside or has spread too far to reach all of it. That diagnosis made perfect sense, even explained why her parents seemed sad a lot of the time and especially why, lately, they were treating her so nicely.

A few weeks after Carly's operation, when he didn't realize Carly saw him, Joel was alone in the spare room, which he used as his study, and the door was practically shut except for a little crack that Carly could see through. Joel didn't make any noise when he cried, just held his head down in his hands and shook for a while. It gave Carly the idea that when boys grow up to be men they're not supposed to make noise anymore when they cry.

Since sooner or later—Carly didn't know how long she had to live—her parents would have to do without her, she wanted to make it as easy on them as she could. She figured it must be especially tough to have your only kid die. She began to behave the way she imagined nuns-in-training and saints behave. Without being asked, she'd empty the dishwasher. Sometimes when she saw Gwen and Joel looking sad and quiet, she'd go get her violin and play Pachelbel's Canon for them.

Carly began to develop the habit of looking for signs. She started imagining that her time to die was getting closer. Sometimes when she was alone, she'd sit very still and listen. She couldn't be sure, but she thought maybe the cancer was beginning to move around and make little sounds. She had to concentrate very hard, which was difficult if there was any noise around her.

She played a game in her head of trying to imagine what would be the worst way to die. She wondered if cancer was worse than lying in bed at night alone with your mother and father out of the house and an axe murderer coming in your window, or worse than being tied to a tree and starved, stabbed, and burned all at once.

When she gets tired of remembering all this, Carly goes over to her desk and opens the drawer where she placed the organ donor form she picked up at the hospital. As she begins to examine it, Carly feels herself well up with energy and purpose.

She opens a pen, places a bold check mark by each entry in the column for vital organs, and imagines a little kid from the children's floor being made miraculously well after receiving the gift of her healthy organ. Wouldn't it be something if you could just drain all the bad blood with all the messed-up cells that course through some sick little girl with leukemia's arteries and veins and replace them with fresh new blood that would make her all better?

Carly wonders if a tumorless brain could be transplanted to make a little boy like Richard whole and healthy again. She suddenly realizes Richard's parents weren't there when he was covered with a sheet and wheeled off the children's floor. She wonders what they were doing instead—she hopes they were together—and tries to imagine what they felt like when the hospital called to tell them the news.

And how about eyes? Could Carly's eyes give her mother's patient Daniel sight? And if you have another person's eyes, do you see things the same way they do? After entering her name, age, address, and the date, Carly is finished with the application. She opens the desk drawer, and as she hides the filled-out donor form under some pads and a pile of blank paper, she finds a few sheets of stickers of little kids with cats and dogs and all sorts of everyday objects that she has had since she was a little girl. Carly thinks of the letter Germaine wrote and illustrated for her grandmother and decides to take the sheets of stickers to the children's floor in the morning.

Just before falling off to sleep, Carly remembers Mary Ellen from camp and how she got down and prayed each night before bed. Saying prayers isn't Carly's thing, but she makes a silent wish for Germaine to get well so she can go home again.

CHAPTER SIXTEEN

On Sunday when she gets up, Carly takes the crosstown bus at 97th Street to the West Side, uses the transfer slip to travel north along the Hudson River, and gets off at 112th Street, where Joel lives in a brownstone between Riverside Drive and West End Avenue.

Even though her parents told her the separation is a mutual decision, Carly assumes that when her mother found out about Edwin, she decided to get a divorce. She imagines her father in some sad and shabby place with junky old furniture and unmatched pots and pans, living a disorganized and tentative life, as though he just received a set of unexpected transfer orders.

Her father's building has no elevator, so Carly walks up four flights to reach his apartment on the top floor. The first thing Carly notices when Joel opens the door is a large, square oil painting propped against the foyer wall. Patches of white and green blur before her, with a slash of dark brown and a rush of bright red, like a bleeding sore oozing across the center of the canvas.

"A new acquisition?" Carly asks as Joel kisses her cheek and closes the door behind her.

"It's the work of a hot young painter working out of a co-op in SoHo. He was just written up in *Art in America* last month, but I found him before he was discovered."

"Nice," Carly says, even though she finds the painting ugly. She walks over to the window on the far side of the apartment, puzzling out the irony of how a person can be found but not yet discovered. It occurs to her that Edwin could be lurking some-where in the apartment—maybe hiding in a closet or under the bed—and Carly has to suppress an urge to flee.

From the living room window, which faces south, Carly can see all the way across town to the Annenberg tower of Mount Sinai Hospital on Fifth Avenue and 101st Street. It rises high above the surrounding buildings and looms beyond the sea of trees in Central Park like a lighthouse marking the way to land. Carly wonders if Joel notices and if when he does he thinks of Gwen, whose office is on the twenty-fourth floor.

Contrary to her expectations, Joel's apartment looks premed-itated and permanent. Her father has begun acquiring things, collecting antique rugs and a certain kind of German/Austrian furniture made out of orangey-colored wood that, Joel tells her, is designed by some guy called "Biedermeier" and dates from the first half of the nineteenth century.

"There are only so many pieces of this kind in the world," Joel tells her, "and because of their scarcity, they're very valuable."

Carly wonders how long it has taken for her father to col-lect so much stuff and considers the possibility that he has been planning for this new life for a very long time.

The chairs are particularly uncomfortable to sit on, and the desk looks way too delicate to use. Joel has placed a leather mat with royal-blue blotter paper on the gleaming surface so nothing will hurt it.

It's a little after noon now, and Carly asks Joel what time the new Woody Allen movie they've planned to see goes on.

"There's a two o'clock and a four o'clock at the Embassy Theatre on Broadway, but I need to hang around until Brian Waterfall comes. He's the guy who did the new painting, and he said he'd stop by sometime this afternoon to sign it."

Carly and Joel eat sandwiches at the new cocktail table, a smoked-glass oval set on a black wrought iron base that has a sculpted snake curled around one of its legs. Two tiny brass balls—the snake's eyes—stare up at Carly as she eats her ham and cheese on rye.

"So tell me what happened at camp," Joel says.

"How about you tell me about what happened to our family?"

Joel looks so stunned and hurt by what she said that Carly decides to backpedal. Staring at the snake's eyes rather than looking at her dad, she says, "You can't even imagine what a shithole place it was. I'm glad I got kicked out. I wanted to get out of there from the minute I arrived."

"Do you think that's why you got in trouble?"

"I got in trouble 'cause I got lost on a trail, and they didn't believe I didn't do it on purpose."

"And did you get lost, or did you do it on purpose?"

"I thought Mom's job was being the shrink."

"We both care about you, Carly, and want to understand what happened so we can help."

"Well, if you really cared, you should've never sent me to a place like that in the first place." Carly can hear her voice getting louder. "And how come if you wanna be so helpful, you didn't let me come home?"

"Your mom felt it would be best to finish out the summer."

"'Cause you'd already paid for it, or 'cause you were blowing up our family and didn't want me around?"

"That's not fair, Carly. You know we both love you."

"Fuck fair!" Carly has begun to scream. "You think coming

home from camp and finding out our family's all fucked up is fair?"

Carly wants to keep screaming and hurling angry words at him, but the shock on her father's face turns her rage to tears and she convulses in sobs.

Joel gets up from where he's sitting and comes over to Carly's side of the cocktail table. "Hey, Squirrelkin, we never meant to hurt you. I'm so sorry your mom and I are having problems." He reaches out a hand to stroke her cheek, but Carly swats it away.

"Stop it, Dad."

Joel collects their plates and goes into the kitchen. He returns with a bottle of Windex and a paper towel and vigorously sprays and wipes the tabletop.

"It's not a Giacometti," Joel says, as he pats the smooth glass surface as though it's a pet dog, "but it's an excellent adaptation by an Israeli sculptor. One of a kind." Carly gets the impression her dad's trying to distract her from her anger by talking about the table.

By the time Brian Waterfall rings the doorbell at quarter to four, Carly and Joel are lying head to foot on either side of the sofa in the living room, trading sections of the Sunday *Times*. Carly hasn't actually been able to concentrate on reading anything, but it has felt good—a little like the way things used to be—to hang out again this way with her dad.

At the sound of the bell, Joel jumps to his feet and rushes to the door as though he has been startled out of a deep sleep. To Carly he seems unusually nervous.

Brian Waterfall wears painter's pants and canvas sneakers splattered with paint. His dark brown hair hangs down his neck and curls over the top of his black turtleneck sweater. A thin paintbrush is tucked behind one ear. Every few seconds he runs long, graceful fingers from the hand that's not holding a tiny can of paint through the clump of hair that falls forward over one eye. Without a word of greeting or introduction, he struts across the apartment and looks out the window.

"Good light," he says to no one in particular. "Southern exposure is always good. Too bad about that rusty nail they ruined the East Side skyline with."

"Yeah, well," Joel says with a nervous half laugh/half cough, "when your name is Annenberg, you want to make it show."

Carly has never heard the Annenberg tower referred to as a rusty nail before. She can't help taking it as a personal insult. It especially bothers her that her dad doesn't say anything to defend it.

Joel puts an arm around Brian's shoulder and ushers him ceremoniously over to where his painting is propped against the foyer wall. Joel is much shorter than Brian Waterfall, and he looks awkward raising up his arm and hitching it over Brian's shoulder. Joel's graying hair is longer than it was before and hangs down in clumps behind his ears and along the back of his neck. The new growth accentuates the top of his head, where the hair is thinning and pink scalp shows through.

Brian tilts his head to one side and cradles his angular, jutting chin with the same hand that he borrows every few moments to sweep back his hair. For what seems like the longest time, he stands there in the foyer studying his painting. The way he looks at it and the expression on his face make Carly wonder if he has ever seen it before. For a brief, agonizing moment she's afraid he's going to tell them that this is all one big mistake, that it's not his painting after all.

"OK," he says finally, as though he has judged and approved the piece of work before him. With a gesture so brisk that it could be sleight of hand, he pulls the paintbrush from behind his ear, dips it in the can of paint, slashes a black line across the center of the painting, and scrawls his signature in the lower right corner.

Joel's smiling mouth drops open and a gasp escapes, and Carly realizes that Brian Waterfall has done something violent. She's horrified.

"What have you done?" Joel demands.

"It was necessary," Brian says definitively in a deep and steady baritone. "For the balance, you know."

Joel's voice cracks like an adolescent boy's. "I liked it the way it was."

Brian closes the cap on the can of paint, wipes the brush on a cloth that hangs from a loop on his painter's pants, and marches toward the door. Joel trails behind, angry and bewildered and more helpless than Carly has ever seen him.

"But it's mine. It's my painting, and you've changed it," Joel whines. "I bought it the way it was, not the way it is now. I want it changed back immediately."

But it's over. Already, Brian has his long, graceful fingers on the doorknob, executes a little ceremonious bow, and leaves.

"It's irrevocable, Mr. Klein," Carly hears him say as the door closes. "It's necessary, believe me, for the balance."

And he's gone.

By now they've missed the four o'clock showing of the Woody Allen film. With nothing left to look forward to, Carly feels like the last drop of hope for today has gone out the door with Brian Waterfall.

"Son-of-a-bitch egotistical artist thinks he can get away with anything. Babies," Joel mutters. "That's what these self-indulgent kids are. A bunch of babies."

She knows he's talking about Brian Waterfall, but Carly can't help feeling she's included in the blame.

When Joel finally stops pacing angrily back and forth before the freshly signed canvas and ranting about what Waterfall has done, he asks Carly if she'd like to go get dinner at a local Chinese restaurant. Carly's not the slightest bit hungry—they just had sandwiches a couple hours ago—but there's nothing else left to do with the day, so she agrees. She is relieved that she didn't have to see Edwin, and now she just wants to get the visit over with.

They're sitting opposite each other at a window table at the Hunan Balcony on upper Broadway when Joel asks Carly if she's losing weight. She keeps looking out the window and onto the street, hoping that by some incredible coincidence her mother's blind patient Daniel, who lives in the neighborhood, will come walking by.

"Just growing, I think," Carly tells him, and continues to turn over pieces of General Tso's chicken with her chopsticks.

"You look thinner," Joel says, staring with squinty eyes, the way he looks when he's concentrating on a difficult matter to figure out.

"It must be what I'm wearing." Carly has on a loose, oversized black T-shirt over black jeans.

Outside on the sidewalk, two men are arguing loudly in Spanish, their arms flying around in wild gestures as they hurl insults at each other. Carly's Spanish takes her only far enough to catch a word or phrase every now and then, but she can tell the men are angry.

Joel finishes off the rest of the chicken and eyes the shrimp with lobster sauce. He holds an overflowing spoonful over Carly's plate and asks if she wants some.

"No thanks," Carly says. "I've still got plenty here to keep me busy."

Her plate is as full as it was when she helped herself fifteen minutes ago, except now the food has been rearranged several times. Before he pulls the serving spoon away, some of the lobster sauce drips onto the chicken on Carly's plate.

"Sorry," Joel says, jerking the spoon away so fast that some more sauce spills on the table.

"Don't worry about it," Carly tells him. "I'm pretty full already."

"Another Coke?" Joel offers, but the first one, which Carly stirs around with a straw, is still almost full.

She lodges a chunk of chicken between two chopsticks, dips it in the duck sauce, and sets it down on the other side of her plate. Outside, the two men have begun to shove each other as they continue to argue. Their voices are getting louder, and a small group of onlookers gathers around. One of the men slugs the other one, whose face fills with blood.

Joel puts his chopsticks down and looks directly at Carly. "Do you think you could tell me what's on your mind?"

"Can't you see? There's a fight going on outside, Dad!"

Finally, Joel turns his attention to the scene, and as he takes in what has happened, he cries out, "Oh my God. Someone get help!"

A waiter rushes over to their table and puts a hand on Carly's shoulder—she's coughing and trying to clear her throat—and shouts, "She's choking! Who can do a Heimlich?"

"It's not me," Carly manages between coughs. "It's them," she sputters, pointing at the scene outside. Embarrassed, the waiter drops his hand from Carly's shoulder to her full plate of food.

"I don't think we're finished yet," Joel tells him.

"I guess I am," Carly says to the waiter, and then to Joel, "All that blood makes me nauseous."

When the waiter brings the check, he places a plate with cut oranges and fortune cookies between them on the table. While

Joel gets out his credit card and figures the tip on the form the waiter has left on a brown plastic tray, Carly cracks open her cookie and examines the fortune. *You will soon meet an exciting stranger who will change your life.* She slips it in the pocket of her jeans and leaves the cracked hull of the cookie on her napkin as she and Joel rise to leave.

"Wanna walk me to the bus?" Carly asks Joel, both hoping to distract him from the cheerless mood but wanting to get away. He digs in his pocket and pulls out a five-dollar bill.

"Maybe you'd better take a cab. It's kind of late."

Joel sticks his arm up in the air, and a cab with a light on top skids to a halt beside them. Carly takes the bill and kisses him goodbye as Joel opens the cab door.

"This was fun," Joel says. "Let's do it again soon."

Carly wouldn't exactly call the afternoon they've just spent "fun," but to make her getaway feel comfortable, she reaches up for a last hug. "Thanks, Dad. See ya soon."

"Love you, Squirrelkin."

CHAPTER
SEVENTEEN

After finishing her shift at the hospital, Carly decides she'll walk across Central Park and hang out around Columbia. When Carly gets to 116th and Broadway, she sees a phone booth on the corner and fishes around in her pocket for a quarter. She still knows Daniel's number by heart, and as she works up her confidence to make the call, she thinks of Lauren accusing her of always wimping out and daring her to do it.

Across the street, on a bench in the middle of the island separating the southbound and northbound sides of Broadway, an old Black man sits wrapped in a dirty blanket. He looks like all the color has been scared out of his frizzy white hair.

In front of him is a makeshift table—a slab of plywood propped up by two crates—on which sits a long wooden xylophone with different colored metal keys. Carly realizes this is kind of a homeless workstation, this island with benches with broken slats and a few scraggly trees and a horde of pigeons clucking and rooting around for crumbs.

When Carly was young, maybe six or seven, she had her own wooden xylophone with different colored metal keys and a little wood stick with a round knob that she used to sound the notes.

She could pick out "Hot Cross Buns" and "Twinkle Twinkle Little Star," and she could create tinkly arpeggios by running the knob of the stick, like a paintbrush, up and down the keys.

What's making Carly the most nervous is how she'll sound on the phone. Her biggest fear is that her voice will give her away, and Daniel will know she's just a high school kid.

Carly finally works up her courage, inserts the quarter in the slot, and dials Daniel's number: 874-1804. Each number triggers a musical note, creating a tune that Carly imagines picking out on a xylophone. The phone rings three times before Daniel picks up. His voice is different from how Carly remembers it, a little more clipped, more grown-up.

"Hello," Carly says fast before she loses her nerve and hangs up. "My name is Serena, and I saw your ad for a reader at the U. Store." She pauses, then blurts out, "It was a while ago, like last spring, but I was wondering if you're still looking for someone."

She waits nervously for Daniel to respond.

"That's great," Daniel says. He sounds genuinely pleased. "Are you a student around here?"

It's one of the questions Carly was expecting, and she's prepared with an answer: "I'll be a sophomore at Barnard in the fall."

"Have you chosen a major yet?"

Carly knows about majors and that everyone in college has to choose one, but she hadn't given a thought to what she would say if Daniel asked this question. She also realizes, with a surge of fear as she gropes for an answer, that choosing a major has to do with what you want to be in life, and Carly doesn't have a clue.

"Are you there?" Daniel is asking. "Serena?"

Carly realizes she has let too much time go by before answering. It feels really strange to hear herself called Serena.

"Art. I'm gonna major in art. I'm a painter."

"Cool," Daniel says, and Carly realizes she has made a safe

choice, because Daniel won't be able to see what she paints and won't know she isn't very good at it.

"How would you feel about reading Mozart's correspondence? I'll be working on a paper for my senior thesis, and I need to examine the family letters."

Carly had no idea that Mozart wrote letters to his family that are printed somewhere that people can read, but she tells Daniel in her most mature, serious-sounding voice, "That sounds very interesting." And then because she's not quite sure how well this interview is going, she adds enthusiastically, "I've always wanted to read Mozart's correspondence."

Apparently, this is the right thing to say, because Daniel asks her right away, "When would you like to start?"

When Carly thought about this conversation ahead of time, she imagined Daniel telling her when he would like her to come, not the other way around.

"Oh, any time is fine," Carly says, and then corrects herself and adds, "Except mornings, when I have a job." She likes the idea of calling what she does at the hospital a "job," which sounds more grown-up than just being a summer volunteer.

"Would tomorrow afternoon be too soon? Or would you rather schedule for another day, Serena?"

There it is again, the strange-familiar name of Serena. Carly wonders if she can get used to being called anything other than Carly.

"Tomorrow afternoon would be fine, perfect." Carly's heart is thumping against the walls of her chest, and the phone booth feels much too hot and confining. "I could be there by one or so," she says into the receiver, barely believing how bold she's being. It's as if she's being wafted along effortlessly on a wave of external energy, like a magic carpet. Carly can't wait to report her bravery to Lauren.

When Daniel says, "Let me give you my address," Carly realizes, horrified, that she almost let on that she already knows where he lives.

Outside the phone booth, on the island in the middle of Broadway, the old Black man is beginning to gather up his belongings. Carly wonders where the man goes when he leaves here and if he plays his xylophone wherever he goes.

Carly thinks of the night she saw her father and Edwin at the Downunder Café when Daniel was playing his gig, and it occurs to her that he and her dad are practically neighbors on the Upper West Side, which means she has to be careful.

Suddenly, she gets an idea and rifles through the Yellow Pages, hanging from a chain in the phone booth, until she sees "Wigs and Hair Pieces." She finds a shop on West Forty-Sixth Street that advertises wholesale prices. With nothing else to do, she decides to spend the afternoon checking it out.

When she finally finds the place, the salesman is a big, fat man whose shirt gapes between buttons, revealing dark swirls of hair pasted against rubbery pink flesh. He makes Carly want to turn and leave. But more than this, she wants to accomplish what she came for, which took two buses and a long, confusing walk. The trip lasted nearly an hour and a half, at least fifteen minutes of which was spent weaving in and out of racks hung with plastic-wrapped dresses rolled at breakneck speed through the streets of what Carly realized must be the "Garment District."

When Carly tells the salesman what she wants, he tells her, "We sell exclusively to the trade. Sorry, dahling." Except for the low voice, he has the same exact accent as her camp counselor Rhona from Roslyn.

Carly doesn't know exactly what "to the trade" means, but she understands he's not keen on selling her a wig. If she's going to change his mind, she has to think fast and come up with a convincing reason.

The image of Germaine from the children's floor at Mount Sinai Hospital comes to mind, and Carly blurts out that she has cancer and is starting chemo treatments and will soon be losing all her hair. The expression on the salesman's face changes so fast, Carly is scared that maybe she has gone too far.

Within a few minutes Carly is sailing out the door, her bushy red hair tied up in a plastic clip and covered with a long, dark wig that falls free in wavy ridges halfway down her back. She looks like her mother's skinny patient Annelies, the one who makes herself vomit after meals.

"You take care now, dahling," the salesman calls after her.

He has given her the hair clip as a "little gift," plus a 10 percent discount on the sale, which makes Carly feel guilty about her lie. She decides to take the subway back uptown. It goes much faster than the bus trip down, and the wig makes her feel much braver than usual. She gets out of the subway at 110th Street, and as she walks along upper Broadway, a "Help Wanted" sign in a health food co-op on 113th Street catches her eye. Checking her reflection in the window, Carly feels a surge of self-confidence and walks in.

The woman who runs the co-op has steel-gray hair parted down the middle and pulled back so tight that her skin looks stretched across her forehead and scalp. She's standing over a stove, stirring a boiling pot of chickpeas with one hand and holding a telephone receiver in the other. Carly catches bits and pieces of a conversation about an inspection permit and a deadline. The woman is obviously angry at the person she's speaking to. She says in a voice loud enough to carry across the store, "Well, if you think you can walk all over someone's right to operate a private business, then you've got another think coming," and bangs down the phone. "Male chauvinist pigs, all of them," the woman says, as if the air in front of her were a person.

She looks up finally and notices Carly, who is embarrassed to be witnessing a stranger's display of anger.

"I saw your ad in the window," Carly begins haltingly, "and I thought, and I wondered if maybe you needed someone to help out—"

"Well, why on earth else would I hang a 'Help Wanted' sign?"

Carly feels about ten years old. Not wanting to say anything more ridiculous than what she has already said, she stands there shifting her weight from one foot to the other.

"Well, don't just stand there," the woman tells her irritably. "Take this and start stirring, and we'll see if you're any good."

She sticks the wooden spoon out toward Carly as though she's pointing a gun at her. Carly takes it and hesitates before walking around the counter to the back side. She hadn't intended to begin work right this very moment, but before she knows it she's standing there, stirring chickpeas.

"Aren't you going to take off your jacket and put your bag down?" the woman asks her, but now she's smiling, as though Carly has passed some invisible test. "And we'd better do something about all that hair, honey."

She grabs a calico scarf from the shelf behind her and hands it to Carly.

"Tie it up with this to keep it out of the food. Health code regulations and all that hooey."

The thickness and heaviness of her new head of hair gives Carly an earthy feeling as she ties back her new long, wavy wig in a big, bunchy ponytail.

"I'm Ruth," the woman tells her, and reaches out to shake Carly's hand. It's a bit awkward, because Carly's holding the wood spoon in her right hand.

"Oh, hell, let's skip the formalities," Ruth says. "Glad to have you on board."

"My name's Serena. I'll be a sophomore at Barnard in the fall," Carly begins to explain, as though she's being interviewed.

"It doesn't matter to me if you're a dolphin from Disneyland. Credentials don't interest me so long as you can chop vegetables and stir a boiling pot. I pay five dollars and fifty cents an hour. No paperwork. Just straight cash. When the bathroom in back needs wiping up, you do that too. I need four hours a day. You want mornings or afternoons?"

"Afternoons after my job reading to a blind student at Columbia could work," Carly tells her, breaking into a smile for the first time. Even though she's doing all this stuff on the sly, Carly thinks her mom might be proud of her for being so grown-up and responsible and having real work jobs.

"Well, for now you just keep stirring, Serena from Barnard, while I go fetch some supplies from my apartment upstairs. Watch that you don't let the chickpeas stick to the bottom of the pot." She winks at Carly as she says, "I'll expect you tomorrow after you help that blind guy see the light," before heading upstairs.

Dear Carly,

That's so incredibly cool about getting a wig—can you send me a photo?—and taking a pseudonym. Serena's a great choice for a name. So "Serene." LOL. That's an acronym for laughing out loud that's creeping into usage on the Internet. And it's awesome that you've signed on as Daniel's reader. I hope that's not ALL you guys do when you get together. He's such a hottie. "Carpe diem," Tibou always says when I procrastinate. Seize the day! And be sure to write me all about it!
XOXO Lauren

CHAPTER EIGHTEEN

I t must be Mozart that fills the air with music, Carly figures as Daniel lets her into his apartment. Of course, she hasn't a clue as to what piece by Mozart, but she thinks it's safe to venture, "Mozart, right?"

When Daniel tells her, "*Don Giovanni*," Carly is momentarily taken aback, but then Daniel adds, "Mozart's greatest opera, don't you think?" and Carly is relieved.

Remembering the music class she followed Daniel to last spring, Carly ventures, "I took Professor Pietro's class last semester."

"Hey, what a coincidence. So did I. He's awesome, don't you think?"

"Yeah, he's very funny. I loved his story about seeing the *Mona Lisa* on roller skates."

"Right," Daniel says. "And the one about getting lost from his family in the Prado in Madrid was a riot."

Carly doesn't want to let on that she didn't hear that story because she wasn't there that day. Instead, she changes the subject.

"So, that's cool you've decided on Mozart for your senior thesis."

An unmade futon occupies most of the floor space, and a

cluttered desk is placed under the single window. Daniel's walls are covered with huge collage-type posters plastered with linear blobs of clay painted black.

"I see you go in for abstractions," Carly observes as she looks around.

"You mean my braille posters? I'm going for a patent. This one"—Daniel waves his hand toward a triangular construction over his bed—"is an anti-nuclear protest, and the one over by the door is a save-the-whales poster. Have a seat. Anywhere is fine."

Carly settles herself onto a corner of the blue-and-white-striped futon. She likes the way Daniel lives in one big room where the bed and the workspace and everything is all together. It seems very cool and casual, and Carly makes a mental note that when she has a place of her own someday, she wants it to be something like Daniel's apartment.

"Want some tea or coffee?"

"You don't have to bother," Carly says, but Daniel is already connecting up an electric teapot, which sits on a little table across the room, and preparing two mugs with tea bags.

"No bother," he tells her. "I was about to fix some for myself."

Carly watches Daniel maneuver around with an obvious sense of familiarity. To watch him here, in his private place, is like watching the way fish move in water, following the current and changing direction by instinct.

"Do you live on campus?" Daniel asks.

"I'm actually a commuter. I live at home," Carly tells him, and then thinks of her dad's apartment and adds, "on the Upper West Side."

The lies are coming easier than Carly expected. If only she can remember the stories she's telling so she can keep them straight.

When the kettle begins to whistle, Daniel asks her, "You'll join me in a cup of tea, won't you?"

Carly doesn't even know she had it in her, but she's feeling freed up by now and quips back, "Think there's room for both of us in the same cup?"

Without missing a beat, Daniel answers, "I guess that depends on how big you are."

The two of them burst out laughing, as though what they're saying is the funniest thing they've ever heard. When Carly finally catches her breath, she gets up and crosses the room, goes right up to him and gives him a gentle nudge. "Move over and make room. I'm gonna join you in your cup of tea." Then they both dissolve in laughter again.

When they've settled down with their tea—Carly on the corner of the futon where she sat before, and Daniel on the floor with his back against a wall—he picks up a book and says, "Here's the first volume of the correspondence. I guess the place to begin is at the beginning."

The light in the room is very dim, and Carly thinks turning on a lamp might help, but she doesn't see one anywhere. She spots an overhead fixture on the ceiling, but she assumes the switch is over by the door, and she doesn't want to spoil the atmosphere by getting up and switching on the light.

Daniel lies on his back on the floor, listening as Carly reads. Beacon lies nearby, curled around himself in a semicircle that gently expands and contracts.

"This one's from Mozart's father to Mozart and his mother when they went to Salzburg on tour," Carly announces, and then begins to read. "*After you both had left, Nannerl wept bitterly . . .*" Carly pauses to ask, "Who's Nannerl?"

"Mozart's sister. That was actually her nickname. Her given name was Maria Anna. And she wrote and played music too."

"I bet they called her Nanny. Like in the movie *Amadeus*, did you see that? Mozart's wife called him Wolfie, pronounced

'Volfie.' I thought it was so cute every time she did that. Anyway . . ."

Carly suddenly realizes Daniel can't actually "see" movies and feels foolish to have asked. She quickly reopens the book and continues reading:

> "After you both had left, Nannerl wept bitterly and I had to use every effort to console her. She complained of a headache and a sick stomach and in the end she retched and vomited; and putting a cloth round her head, she went off to bed and had the shutters closed. When I came in with the dog, I woke Nannerl and ordered lunch. But she had no appetite, she would eat nothing and went to bed immediately afterwards . . ."

Carly stops reading and comments, "She sounds like a real neurotic. What do you think her problem was?"

"It's obvious, she missed them."

Carly gets a thought and sits straight up. "You just told me Mozart's sister played piano and gave concerts and composed music."

"Yeah, and she even went on tour when she was younger."

"So why'd she stop?" Carly asks indignantly. "And how come Mozart got to continue?"

She has begun to sound angry, as though she's fused with the victim and feels compelled to defend her.

Daniel rolls onto his stomach and props himself up on his elbows. "Because Mozart was a boy, and this was eighteenth-century Europe. There was no such thing as professional female musicians or composers in those days."

"I bet Nanny secretly hated Volfie's guts and was really jealous and pissed off that he got trucked all around and that she had to stay home 'cause she was just a girl."

Beacon snores and startles awake, as though something intrusive has entered his dream.

"That's incredible, Serena," Daniel tells her. "Feminist historians would lose it over a theory like that. It's ingenious."

"And you know what else? You know that business about her not being hungry and not eating anything and retching? I bet she was secretly anorexic too."

Carly hears her own voice, filled with self-confidence, and is amazed. She feels like she's on some kind of high that just keeps going. "I bet when she didn't like what was going on, she'd stick her finger down her throat and make herself vomit."

By the time Carly leaves, she and Daniel have set a schedule for a couple hours per afternoon, five days a week, Monday through Friday. When Carly gets downstairs, she checks her watch and sees that it's after three o'clock. She can't believe how fast the time has gone and how much fun it is being Daniel's reader. When she gets home, the first thing she plans to do is write Lauren all about it.

CHAPTER NINETEEN

After the first few times Carly reads for Daniel, it feels like hanging out with a friend. She not only reads from the Mozart correspondence, she also reads Daniel's own mail. They talk about lots of stuff and sometimes even go out for walks and coffee. Carly can't be sure because she realizes Daniel hired her and that she's doing a job, but she gets the idea that this is what a real relationship between grown-up girls and guys is like.

Daniel seems to like her a lot, and he has special treats and little gifts for her when she comes. One day he offers yummy blondies from a local bakery along with a cup of hot chocolate. Another day he gives her a small notebook with blank pages. "For your sketches and art notes," he tells her as she opens the bag.

Today, Carly appears at Daniel's door in sneakers and a pair of black tights with an oversized tie-dyed T-shirt that barely covers the tops of her thighs. Her bushy red hair is covered with the long, dark, wavy wig that falls free in kinky ridges down her back.

"Peace," Daniel says as he opens the door to Carly's knock. The index and middle fingers of his right hand form a V.

He has already explained to Carly on other occasions that

his spirit is with the sixties, which he believes were the brightest shining moment in modern American history. Daniel is of the opinion that everything that has happened since—Watergate, the Iran–Contra affair, the Reagan and Bush administrations, the rise of what he calls the "yuppie class"—is a sign of the decadence that always, throughout history, has preceded the decline and fall of civilization. As Carly enters, he goes over to his desk and brings over a tiny box.

"Happy birthday," he tells her, and she looks up in amazement.

"But it's not my birthday," she tells him.

"It doesn't matter," he says, and places a hand on her shoulder as he explains. "Birthdays shouldn't be just for us but to celebrate the truly important events that are born in the world."

When Carly opens the little package, she finds a set of dangly earrings with large silver doves that jingle at the bottom.

"They're beautiful, Daniel. I love them!"

"The peace doves are to celebrate the imminent withdrawal of Vietnam from Cambodia," Daniel explains. Then he leans over and kisses Carly on the mouth, slowly and gently.

Just as she's puzzling out the meaning of the word "imminent," Carly feels Daniel's tongue parting her lips. Not knowing what to do, she opens her mouth slightly, holding her breath. When it's over, Carly can't believe what just happened. She has never been kissed before, but Daniel acts as though what he has just done is the most natural thing in the world.

"How about I make us some tea?" Daniel asks as he pulls away.

He plugs in the teapot, and Carly settles herself on the floor. While they wait for the water to boil, Carly rehearses the letter she'll write Lauren about how much cooler and more experienced Daniel is than Lance, that horrible, horny guy who groped her at the dance at camp.

When Daniel goes over to a ficus tree in the far corner of the room and pinches out some dry, greenish powder from a can at its base, Carly asks, "What are you doing?"

Daniel tells her, in his voice of wisdom that sends chills up her spine, "I'm feeding the tree. It lives and breathes just like we do."

In the time that Carly has been coming to Daniel's room, the ficus tree has lost half its leaves.

"It needs time to adjust," Daniel tells her when she expresses concern, "and to recover, like Vietnam and Cambodia. It will take time for them to learn to be at peace."

Carly is trying to work out the connection between the dying ficus tree and the Vietnamese withdrawal from Cambodia when Daniel carries over their cups and announces that to celebrate, they're going to take a holiday from reading Mozart and instead will read some poetry.

Besides studying music and making braille abstractions, Daniel is a poet and writes the kind of poems that have no rhymes. The books that line his shelves are mostly poetry by people like Anne Sexton and Sylvia Plath. He says he wishes he had lived in the sixties when they lived, so he could feel closer to what it was that caused them to die.

But before reading poetry, Daniel pulls something from his shirt pocket that's wrapped in silver foil paper. He carefully unrolls it, and Carly recognizes a joint, like the ones her counselor Rhona from Red Soil Ranch taught them to smoke. Daniel takes a lighter from his pants pocket and passes it to Carly along with the joint.

"Won't you do the honors?" he asks her.

"Yeah, sure," Carly says, trying to sound as cool as she can.

As the afternoon wears on, Carly and Daniel sit on the floor by the window, pass the joint between them, and take turns reading and reciting verses to one another. The sensation of Daniel's tongue lightly grazing her teeth has stayed with her, and Carly runs her own tongue over her teeth again and again, pretending it's Daniel repeating the kiss.

In between reciting poems, Daniel tells Carly stories about the poets' lives. Everyone who is anyone who writes worthy poetry, it seems, lives a life filled with the worst, most unimaginable pain and suffering. No one lives happily ever after. In fact, no one lives very long, 'cause mostly they all kill themselves.

Daniel thinks the kind of stuff that Carly has been doing in her English class is not only "insipid" but potentially damaging to her "literary integrity." He reacts vehemently to the poem she recites by Alfred Lord Tennyson, the way someone with asthma reacts to dust. Carly doesn't admit she had to memorize it for Ms. Cribben's class at Baxter but just rattles it off as though committing poems to heart comes automatically to her.

Daniel's violent eruption of abuse at her recital of the Tennyson is unlike anything Carly has heard before from him. When she reaches the final couplet, *I hope to see my Pilot face to face / When I have crossed the bar*, Daniel groans.

"Please. Stop. Enough," he says, as though it causes him physical pain.

He tells her the treatment of the death theme is "overworked and sophomoric," and calls the term "pilot" a "pathetically cheap metaphoric shot at God." He groans again and declares, "They should censor stuff like that. I can't imagine anyone assigning bullshit like that in a college course."

Even though Carly's shocked at the suggestion of censoring Alfred Lord Tennyson, she nods in agreement. Then she remembers Daniel can't see her nodding, and tells him, "Yeah, right. It's so high school, anyway."

"Yeah," Daniel agrees, calming down finally.

Carly sees the gentle, approving look he gives her when she

says the right things. Then he leans over and reaches out toward her. The next thing she knows, he's cupping her face with his hand and kissing her again, but this time it's not like before. The way he's pulling her toward him has an urgency, and his tongue in her mouth is moving fast and going deeper as Daniel pushes her down on the floor.

Soon he's lying with his chest on her chest, and she begins to get a squashed, uncomfortable feeling, but she knows it wouldn't be cool to complain. Carly wishes she could stop him and they could rearrange themselves so his weight wasn't pressing down so hard on her. She feels his hand moving higher and higher between her thighs till he's cupping her crotch and rocking his hand gently back and forth. At first Carly tenses, but then she begins to feel the good sensations she coaxes when she rehearses in bed by herself at night.

Just as she begins to relax and ease into the pleasure, Daniel removes his hand and begins fumbling with his belt. She hears his zipper open, and then he's taking her hand and placing it inside his underwear. He covers her hand with his own and circles it around his erection, squeezing tighter as he guides her up and down. Carly hears him groan, almost as though he's hurting, but she knows it's not pain that's coursing unstoppably through him. Daniel cries out, and she feels her hand fill with a warm wetness.

Carly's not sure she likes what has just happened. She knows she shouldn't wipe her hand on the futon but does it anyway. She wonders if Lauren would think it's cool that Daniel came in her hand, or if she'd think they should have gone all the way instead.

The next time Carly checks Gwen's session notes, her heart practically does a somersault when she reads, *D. delighted with new reader, Serena: smart and funny.* Carly was hoping Daniel had talked about what happened, but part of her likes the idea that he doesn't tell his shrink the private, sexy stuff. It makes it kind of like a secret between her and Daniel.

Carly's about to take a swig of milk from the carton to go with some Oreo cookies when Gwen comes into the kitchen.

"How's the volunteer work going with Susan?" Gwen asks.

"Great," Carly tells her, smoothly pouring the milk into a coffee mug. "I really enjoy working with the kids."

"That's wonderful," Gwen says. "Susan says you have a natural way with them."

"You talk to her about me?"

"Well, only once when we passed in the hall."

"Whatever," Carly says as she separates the chocolate wafers and nibbles the white cream filling.

"Don't you think you should have something besides cookies for breakfast?" Gwen pours herself a cup of coffee.

"I eat breakfast with the kids when I get to the hospital. By the way, Lauren asked if I could visit her in Vermont the last weekend in August."

"Over Labor Day?" Gwen asks.

"The weekend before that. They have to leave for California over Labor Day weekend so Lauren and Marc can start school out there."

Carly's annoyed that Gwen is asking all these question that led her to talk about Lauren leaving. She doesn't want to think about that, just about the upcoming visit to Vermont and being with her best friend again.

"Well, we'll have to look into transportation up to Vermont for you."

"Tibou's got it covered. She already sent a bus schedule. I'll check it out."

Gwen stops packing her briefcase with the stack of files she has brought into the kitchen. "Mrs. Lensky already sent you a schedule? Before you even cleared it with me if you could go?"

"What's the big deal?"

"How's Mrs. Lensky's pregnancy going?"

"I guess everything's OK. Lauren hasn't said anything."

Carly's not sure, but she thinks Gwen sounds jealous, maybe even a little sarcastic, when she says, "I suppose Mrs. Lensky has that covered too."

CHAPTER
TWENTY

arly sets out at the crack of dawn and takes a six-and-a-half-hour bus ride to spend the weekend with the Lenskys in Vermont. On the long ride Carly has lots of time to think about things, and even though she wants to feel upbeat and excited about this trip to a new and distant place, she can't help remembering what she has left behind. She misses Daniel practically every minute of every hour, and when she thinks of her broken family, her heart breaks all over again.

The entire Lensky family turns out to pick her up at the depot, and instead of driving straight back to their house in Cabot, Marc announces that they're going on a picnic to celebrate Lauren's birthday.

"Sounds like fun," Carly says as she hugs Lauren hello.

"Not to me it doesn't," Lauren says. "I'm only doing it to indulge Tibou. She thinks picnics are a nearly extinct art form."

"Sounds like Tibou," Carly replies, and right away she feels the good, happy way she always feels when she's with Lauren's family.

Saturday is a magnificent late August day. It's sunny and warm with patches of cool that feel like going underwater and swimming through the cold zones. The leaves are just beginning to take on fall color, but the grass is still deep, velvety green.

At the birthday picnic for Lauren, Tibou's large, rounded belly leads everywhere as she walks—it's more of a duck waddle—and her reddish-gray hair seems more flyaway than ever. Even though they are in the middle of a wilderness, she's still wrapped in the red-and-yellow-checkered apron she always wears at home.

Tibou has packed a picnic lunch in a large straw hamper, but before she unpacks it, Lauren and Carly are instructed to prepare the spot where they'll be eating the meal. Lauren has obviously picnicked before, but the ritual is new to Carly. From the trunk of the car they remove a stack of items that she and Lauren lay out, according to specifications delivered in rapid-fire French that Carly cannot follow: a large plaid blanket, cloth napkins, real silverware, breakable dishes, glasses that Carly recognizes as the handblown ones that were made by someone Tibou refers to as an "artisan" from Greenwich Village.

Tibou empties the straw hamper, and on the ground before them expands the most elaborate picnic spread Carly has ever seen. There's a loaf of crusty bread and wedges and rounds of orange and white cheeses and a bowl full of deep-red grapes and a plate filled with something called "eggs mimosa" that look like deviled eggs but have chopped-up pieces of olive in them. Before they sit down to eat, Tibou announces, "Boys must learn to smell the flowers too," and she sends Marc to collect ferns and wildflowers from the woods.

"Why not send Papa too?" Lauren asks.

"Because Papa works all week, and this is his time to rest."

"Talk about sexist!" Lauren's chest heaves and she sighs loudly, as though she can't bear another moment.

Tibou tells her something in French, and Marc makes a

teasing face at Lauren and announces, "When I'm the papa in my family, I'm gonna make the girls pick the flowers."

"How original," Lauren says, and makes a scornful face.

When Marc returns, Tibou makes a plump bouquet that she sticks in a rotted-out log stump and sets down as the centerpiece for the meal.

"*Ça ressemble à une nature morte de Cézanne*," Tibou announces as she assesses the magnificent arrangement of food and flowers.

"*Nature morte* means 'still life,'" Marc explains. "They call it 'dead nature' in French."

"I thought you didn't like speaking French," Lauren says.

Even though it seems ridiculously morbid, the logic of the idiom fascinates Carly. All through the day the phrase, like a catchy refrain, returns to her. It doesn't seem right to call something dead that's so fully alive. She wishes the French had found a different way of saying it.

After the meal is done, Mr. Lensky naps with his head in his wife's lap. His fluffy black mustache is flecked with powdered sugar from the cake Tibou baked for Lauren's birthday. Tibou reads aloud from a very old, crumbling volume of poems by a French poet named Verlaine. The book has a green strip of ribbon attached to its spine, which serves as a page marker.

Marc whittles away at sticks he finds in the woods with the knife they used to slice bread and cheese. With his pale face framed by a full head of black hair, he looks just like a miniature Mr. Lensky minus the mustache. Lauren draws with a stick Marc has sharpened, carving pictures in the earth. Carly worries they'll be erased by wind or rain, and she is horrified when Lauren smudges everything out with the palm of her hand. For the rest of the afternoon, Carly pretends she's part of the family, living through an episode of *Little House on the Prairie*.

With classical music playing softly on the car radio while Marc sleeps with his head on Tibou's shoulder, they drive home to Cabot through a multicolored sunset smeared across the sky. A piece with piano and violins begins, and Tibou startles the calm with a very loud "Ach," dwelling long and hard on the final sound in that throaty way the French pronounce *ch*'s. "*C'est du Mozart.*"

It pleases Carly the way the *t* is silent and the *z* is soft, like the letter *z* should be, she thinks. And she likes the way Tibou gives equal emphasis to both syllables: MO-ZAR. Carly practices in a whisper and rehearses in her mind how the next time she goes to Daniel's, she'll tell him how the French pronounce the composer's name. As she watches the sun drop below a mountain in the distance, it occurs to Carly that as long as she lives, she'll never forget today.

With their move to California coming in less than a week, Lauren and her family are busy packing things they plan to bring. The cardboard boxes placed all around the house slowly fill with clothes and games.

Tibou is huge now and has swollen ankles and varicose veins in her legs. The baby has settled on a nerve, and every now and then she stops whatever she's doing, clutches the underside of her enormous, bulging belly, and winces in pain. The baby's not due until after Christmas, but Tibou keeps saying, "I don't believe a word of it. Number three babies come fast and easy."

She pronounces the word "three" as though it's spelled *sree*. Mr. Lensky flattens his fluffy mustache with his hand and tells Tibou something in Russian that Lauren translates for Carly's benefit: "Papa thinks Tibou's an incurable optimist."

An Italian opera is playing in the background on the stereo while everyone sits around the living room after dinner. Carly, Lauren, and Marc are playing a game of Monopoly while every now and then Mr. Lensky breaks out in a full-bodied tenor voice that but for the Russian accent comes remarkably close to sounding like the singer in the recording.

"My father could've been an opera star," Marc pipes up proudly. "Only he thought he'd make a bigger contribution to the world by being an architect."

Carly thinks of her own father and can't imagine ever feeling anything like the pride Marc feels for Mr. Lensky. The only thing she can think about when she thinks of her father these days is his being gay, and she can't imagine ever telling anyone about that.

Just as Lauren scores Park Place, Tibou rushes from the room with a shriek she barely muffles against the back of her hand. The whole house launches into a flurry of motion, and Lauren is given a long list of instructions in Russian by her father. Carly knows he's giving instructions because after every few spurts of speech, Lauren tells him, "Yes, I'll do it," and "Yes, I'll be sure."

Within minutes Tibou and Mr. Lensky are gone. Besides the coat that Mr. Lensky has thrown over his wife's shoulders, he wraps the red plaid blanket from the picnic around her as they rush out the door.

"Her water broke," Lauren tells Carly, once the house is quiet and still again. "Tibou was right. The baby's coming early."

With nothing else to do, Carly, Lauren, and Marc settle back down to playing Monopoly, but the fun of buying properties and setting up houses and hotels around the board has gone out of the game.

"It's gonna be a boy, I know it," Marc announces as he moves his Monopoly token to Marvin Gardens. His big black eyes reflect the golden glow from the lamp by which they're playing.

"You don't know that," Lauren tells him. "It's just what you wish."

"It's a free country, and I can wish what I want."

"Whatever," Lauren says, and Carly can tell that even Lauren, who usually takes everything in stride, is upset by what's happening and doesn't know how to react.

Carly waits until they're in bed with the lights out before she tells Lauren about what's been going on with Daniel and how far they've gone. She figures talking about doing stuff with boys will distract Lauren from her worry about Tibou.

Lauren sits bolt upright in bed. "That's so cool! Way to go, girl! Now that you've gone to third base, you can move this thing along."

"Yeah, well, we'll see how it goes."

"What are you doing about birth control?" Lauren asks.

"We're not there yet, Lauren!"

"Well, you have to be prepared," Lauren says as she lies back down and pulls the comforter up around her. "Night night, Carly. Sweet dreams of Daniel."

It's late when Carly awakens. The light that comes in through the window is bright and strong, and for a moment she can't remember where she is. Then she looks over and sees Lauren's empty bed, and the memory of last night and what happened comes flooding back. Carly imagines Tibou rushing out the door, wrapped in the red plaid blanket Mr. Lensky threw around her as they left last night. A phone is ringing somewhere in the house, and someone is moving around in the hall outside the door. After a lull, Lauren enters the room.

"That was my dad on the phone," Lauren says as she plops down on her bed. "He called to let us know that Tibou's doing fine."

"What'd she have?" Carly asks eagerly.

Lauren's mouth twitches slightly, almost not at all, and she tells Carly, "It was stillborn."

Carly has never heard the word and cannot imagine what it means.

"Stillborn?" she asks in bewilderment.

Lauren's voice is trembling when she tells Carly, "The baby didn't make it. He was born dead."

"Why?" Carly hears herself ask, more to herself than to Lauren.

"Who knows why shit happens?" Lauren says as she curls up in a ball facing the wall.

"Will you still move to California?" Carly asks, and once the words are out, she's surprised at her own question.

"Of course," Lauren says, sounding defensive now. "Dad said Tibou'll be up and around in a day or so. Everything's fine."

Carly wonders if Lauren thinks she's being comforting, giving reassurance. She was hoping Lauren would say the plans have changed and now they won't be going away. She thinks of Tibou at the picnic the other day—so active and busy making everything right—and smells the musty damp earth smell of rotting log and wildflowers. She thinks she hears Lauren crying softly in her bed across the room, and she wishes with all her might that instead of what's happening, their last time together before Lauren moves to California could be a happy memory.

As Carly pulls the covers up tight under her chin, she puzzles out the meaning of the word "stillborn": like a still life painting, in a way, of a living, breathing baby dying to be born.

CHAPTER
TWENTY-ONE

When school starts up again in the fall, Carly falls into a pattern. At first she goes to school in the mornings and then drops out after lunch so she can go to her job at the health food co-op before her hours with Daniel. But after the first couple weeks, she just starts skipping school entirely. Instead, she gets up and goes across town to work morning hours with Ruth at the co-op so she can be free to go to Daniel's for the whole afternoon.

After the first few times Carly cuts class, a letter comes home informing her mother of the unexplained absences. Seeing the return address of her school on the envelope with Willoughby Harrington's name above it, Carly intercepts it, tears it up, and flushes the pieces down the toilet.

When the next letter comes, she does the same thing, not even bothering to read it. Carly realizes she has to come up with a way of holding off the barrage of notes from Ms. Harrington. So she cooks up the idea of writing a letter in Gwen's name explaining the absences.

There are only two possibilities, really, to explain being out of school this much, Carly thinks as she formulates the letter in her mind. There's mononucleosis, which someone winds up getting every year, and there are nervous breakdowns, but they're much rarer and more complicated. Carly taps her pencil on her head a few times, making a loud wooden sound, and then decides she's definitely more the mono type.

After writing a first draft in pencil, Carly takes a piece of Gwen's printed stationery and types out the excuse, which takes up half the page, single-spaced. When she rereads what she has written, an achy feeling, like a menstrual cramp, clutches at her somewhere deep down inside. Her own mother, had she written such a letter, could never have sounded so motherly. Even though it's only a forgery, even though the whole premise of this letter is a fake, there's a kind of self-caring in the way she has framed her own case that catches Carly off guard and makes her eyes flood with tears.

In the afternoons Carly spends with Daniel, she's introduced to a whole new world. She inherits Daniel's ready-made circle of friends, mostly Columbia girls who write poems that don't rhyme like the ones Daniel writes and work on the literary magazine. Daniel thinks it's cool that Carly goes to Barnard, which is just for women, and that the best thing that has happened to Columbia College is that it went coed, which just happened a few years ago.

"Women have so much more sensibility than men," Daniel explains.

Gislinde from Germany and Vicki and Naomi, who take Carly in unquestioningly in a way she has never been accepted by her peers, are infinitely more interesting to her than the giggly girls at Baxter who spend their time applying makeup in the bathroom between classes.

After a couple hours of reading Mozart's letters, Carly and Daniel take a walk over to Broadway to grab some coffee at Chock Full o'Nuts, where they run into Naomi and Aaron sitting at the counter sharing a whole-wheat doughnut and sections of the *New York Times*. Carly has a girl crush on Naomi, who's sleeping with Aaron, who's a senior in political science.

Naomi just got word last week that she was chosen to be an intern at NOW, the National Organization for Women, and will be spending next semester in Washington, DC. It has become clear to Carly that in spite of Willoughby Harrington's vests and ties and her rabble-rousing Monday morning assembly addresses, the Baxter School doesn't know beans about real feminism.

Naomi is so self-confident she wears her large, square glasses all the time. Aaron has blond, wavy hair and an apple-cheeked, clear-skinned complexion. He looks like a great big, beautiful choirboy. Carly has seen him on campus from a distance several times, but close-up he's even handsomer than she realized.

"Hey, congratulations on the internship," Daniel tells Naomi. "That's super."

"Thanks. I'm psyched," Naomi says as she reaches across Aaron for the Sunday *Book Review*.

Her arm grazes his cup, and some coffee spills on the counter. Aaron doesn't even stop reading his section of the *Times* as Naomi sops up the coffee with a napkin. It amazes Carly how, if she didn't know, she'd think they were just a couple of friends. She sees no telltale sexual signs or symptoms whatsoever. She decides that this must be what sophisticated, mature people look like when they have sex. That's how she'll look, she resolves, when she has her first affair someday.

"Have you heard anything from the Fulbright Committee?" Naomi asks Daniel.

"Nothing so far," Daniel tells her. "I'll keep you posted."

Carly recognizes the reference to "Fulbright" from Gwen's notes about a fellowship Daniel's applying for in Germany for next year. He hasn't ever mentioned it to her, so she hasn't been able to ask him about it. Now that Naomi has brought it up, Carly makes a mental note to ask Daniel about it later.

"Hey, if you don't have a class, how about coming with us, Serena?" Aaron asks as he hops off his stool. "We're just heading over to Kennedy's Nineteenth-Century British Novel. He's awesome."

"I've got this," Naomi says, picking up the check and pulling out some bills to pay for the coffee and doughnuts.

"That sounds cool," Carly says, flattered to be asked, hoping it's OK with Daniel, who also takes this class, if she tags along.

"Yeah, you'd like Kennedy. He's a real trip," Daniel says, and it's settled.

As boring and uninspiring as Carly finds Baxter, college fascinates her. One big difference, she notices, between high school and college is that professors use expressions like "as it were" and "indeed" as though they were part of normal speech. Carly tries these out in casual conversation with Daniel from time to time. She gets the impression this is perfectly natural. But the one time she forgets herself with her mother and finishes a sentence with "as it were," Gwen looks startled.

It gets to be a regular thing that Carly attends Kennedy's class along with Naomi, Aaron, and Daniel. Even though she's not technically taking the course, when the professor announces that papers are due at the end of the month, Carly decides to write on *Tess of the d'Urbervilles*, which she read last year when it was on Baxter's required summer reading list.

"I think I'll have a shot at a 'feminist reading' of *Tess*," she tells Daniel after class as they're walking to his apartment.

"That's awesome," he says, and seems even more excited about Carly's project than his own on mausoleum imagery in George Eliot's *Middlemarch*, which he has been listening to on tape. Carly doesn't say so, but she thinks Daniel's choice of subject sounds creepy.

Carly spends the next week working harder than she has ever worked in her life. She underlines in luminescent yellow practically every other line of her tattered copy of *Tess*. She feels propelled by a kind of energy she hasn't had for schoolwork in a very long time, maybe not since she was in elementary school, when she loved the projects they were assigned in class and brought them home proudly to show off to her parents. The paper on *Tess* is a way of proving she's really still the smart, fast learner she was as a little kid when everything came easy to her.

Maybe the challenge of being like the other college kids around her, of sounding like they sound and writing like they write and passing as though she's actually one of them, has set a fire under Carly. It's weird how even though she's cutting school at Baxter, where her grades were falling, here at college she's sitting in on classes and understanding the stuff the professors are saying without any problem.

Carly loves sitting up in her room at her desk with the house all quiet around her, thinking up thoughts to say about the character Tess, whom she has come to think of as a personal friend.

As she works on the paper, nothing her mother does bothers her the slightest bit. Memories flood back of lying in bed with her father when she was a little girl, cuddling in the crook of his arm as he turned pages of the *New Yorker* magazines he read all the time. He would show her the cartoon drawings and ask what she saw when she looked at them. It was like a detective story, figuring out the meaning behind the pictures.

She remembers exactly the moment she first read words that appeared below the drawings, sounding out the syllables and pronouncing them out loud as she traced her finger underneath them. Her father got so excited he called her mother into the room—she was washing up before bed—and Gwen came out with cold cream all over her face to watch Carly read aloud from the magazine for the first time.

Her parents seemed so happy then, happy with her and happy together, that it's hard for Carly to figure out where the happiness went. She knows it faded for a very long time before her parents separated, and now she knows it had to do with her father and Edwin, but she can't pinpoint the time when it went out of their lives, just that everything changed, like the way it feels when clouds come out and cover the sun. Where did it go, the bright, sunny childhood she remembers from long, long ago?

For the first time ever, Carly finishes an assignment before it's due. She tries out a bunch of titles and finally settles for "*Tess of the d'Urbervilles*: Trial and Temptation in the Chase." She reads her pages fresh off the typewriter aloud to herself, over and over again. She's especially pleased with her metaphoric use of "Chase," the name the author, Thomas Hardy, gives to the forest in which young Tess is pursued and raped by her cousin Alec. Carly remembers Lauren saying she was "born to paint" and suddenly thinks, *Hey, maybe I was born to write!* Carly can't wait to send Lauren a copy of her paper.

The next time she's with Daniel, who hasn't lifted a finger to start his own paper, Carly reads him her final draft and is disappointed when he criticizes her interpretation.

"But Tess isn't raped by Alec. She lets him have sex with her."

Carly's careful work on this central question makes her confident, and she tells Daniel, "Submission isn't the same as consent."

"But seducing a woman isn't the same as forcing her to have sex."

"That's why I wrote about trial versus temptation."

"Well, putting Alec on trial for letting him get into her pants isn't exactly fair."

Just as Carly's confidence begins to wobble, Daniel tells her, "Hey, your paper's really good. Too bad you're not taking Kennedy's course for credit. I bet you'd get an A if you were."

"It won't go to waste," Carly tells him.

Daniel has been lying on his back on the floor, and now he gets up and comes over to her on the futon. Carly loves the first part, when Daniel reaches for her and cups her face with his hand and begins kissing her. Sometimes he lies on top of her, pressing his erection against her, and she likes that part too. Her favorite part is when he rocks his hand back and forth on her crotch and makes her tingle, but more and more lately he skips straight to unzipping his pants so she can rub him and make him come.

Today is happening differently, and instead of reaching for Carly's hand when he unbuckles his belt, Daniel stands up, takes off his pants, and tosses them across the floor. When she opens her eyes to see what's going on, he's standing over her, and Carly can see his erection close-up for the first time. It's very big, bigger than she realized when she touched it with her hand, and she's surprised that it's moving a little bit all by itself.

Carly knows what's happening, but her mind is racing to assemble her reaction. She knows she's going to let Daniel go all the way, but a jumble of confusing thoughts—like what they're going to do about birth control and whether she's supposed to take off her clothes—clogs her response. As Daniel lies back down on the futon, Carly thinks of Tess asleep in the forest where Alec takes her by force. Or is it by force?

"Don't worry," Daniel tells her as he lifts her T-shirt and runs a hand over her bra. "I'll take care of everything," he says, unfastening the clasp and cupping her breast as he climbs on top of her.

Carly tenses when she feels Daniel's hand move down inside her panties. Usually, he rubs her from outside her tights. Maybe Daniel's right and Tess consents to Alec's seduction. It's not clear in the story, and now it's not clear in Carly's mind. As Daniel tugs at her tights and panties, she slides into a state of make-believe, imagining she's Hardy's innocent heroine giving in to the more experienced, older man.

As it's happening, this event she has played out in her mind over and over, Carly feels none of the soft, melty feelings she always feels when she rehearses by herself in bed at night. Instead, her body remains stiff and tight, until the piercing little pain when Daniel enters her. As soon as he's inside, a slight tingly sensation takes over, but before she can settle into it, Daniel lifts himself out of her and rolls over on his back. Carly wants to ask if he was using protection, but she feels too shy.

"It gets better the more you do it," he reassures her. "You should've told me you were a virgin. I would've gone slower."

"That's OK," Carly tells him in a small, high voice like a child's.

The feeling of being Tess has left her, and now she's herself again, thinking of Lauren doing it with Elliott. *It was cool,* Lauren wrote in her letter. Carly's not sure how she'd describe doing it with Daniel, but "cool" isn't it. Maybe she won't describe it, just mention casually that it happened.

Before Carly leaves for the day, Daniel gives her a set of keys and permission to come over if she needs a place near campus to kill time between classes.

"You could bring some art supplies," Daniel tells her, "if you want to work on your painting."

In her next letter to Lauren, Carly decides, she'll tell about the keys and the invitation to come over and paint. She's not so sure anymore about sending the paper, and she's not at all sure about what she feels about the rest of what happened. Maybe when she figures it out, maybe after the next time, which Carly hopes will be different and a whole lot better, she'll let Lauren know.

TWENTY-TWO

J ust as her hours at the health food co-op are about to end, the door opens with a jangle from the set of bells that hangs from the inside knob, and two girls come in and walk over to the counter.

"Can I get some hummus with a pita?" the one with the Barnard sweatshirt asks Carly, then turns to her friend and says, "What'd you think of Taylor's lecture?"

"The usual vacuous bullshit," the other one, who's short and stocky with a buzz cut and torn jeans, replies. "I couldn't believe how he summed the whole thing up to Hamlet wanting to leave home and his mother not wanting to let him go. It's so reductive."

She doesn't look up at Carly when she asks, "Can I get some falafel? I'll take that in a pita. And an iced tea."

Carly rings up the total on the cash register, the way Ruth has shown her how to do. "That'll be ten fifty."

"I'll take a Diet Coke," the girl in the sweatshirt says, and then turns to her friend. "*Hamlet's* overrated anyway."

Carly hands her the Coke and says, "Eleven twenty-five."

The girls fumble around for the correct money, and the short, stocky one collects a fistful of change from her friend and pays. As they carry off their trays, Carly feels a surge of indignation. The nerve of them not even saying thanks.

When she's done for the day at the health food co-op, it's only noon, and Daniel's in class till later this afternoon, so Carly has lots of time to kill before they meet back at the apartment. She decides to use her earnings to buy some paint supplies. She goes to an art store a few blocks away on Amsterdam Avenue and selects a few brushes and some primary colors.

She remembers herself as a little girl, standing in the corner of her bedroom in front of her little wooden easel with the narrow tray at the bottom lined with jars of poster paints: red, blue, yellow, black, white. All the other colors she needed could be mixed from these. It was like a language learned long ago that Carly knew from when she played with finger paints, that red mixed with blue gives purple and that blue and yellow make green. If you need brown, as in tree trunks or for the earth, you combine red and black.

Carly scans the row of little tubes of color and decides to add some of her recent favorites like "burnt ochre" and "cerulean blue" to the primary colors she has already selected. Earth and sky colors, Carly thinks as she holds the tubes of acrylic in her hand and calculates whether she can afford the basic wood easel that she sees set up across the store. It's OK, she figures, if she uses up her whole paycheck on this stuff. She still gets an allowance from her mother, and she needs very little to get by, since Ruth lets her eat whatever she likes when she comes to work.

Carly uses the keys Daniel gave her to let herself into his apartment. She moves the ficus tree, which by now has lost all its leaves, and sets up her easel by the window. She knows Daniel's in class and won't be returning until two hours from now, so she has enough time to get something going. The first thing she does is prepare a palette from the cardboard backing to the pad of paper. She sets up little mounds of color in a semicircle and then starts to think of what she wants to paint.

The moment before committing paint to blank paper is always terrifying: once she makes her move, Carly knows, it's impossible to unmake it. She takes a brush and begins to dab samples of color onto the paper she has posted on her easel. The burnt ochre, a mustardy tone, is darker than she expected, and for no reason in particular she swooshes some white through it until it comes up more yellowy gold, like the hayfields and sunflowers in Van Gogh's paintings. It feels like fun, this swooshing around randomly with no specific plan in mind.

More boldly now, Carly swirls paint around, first in just an upper corner and then downward in a triangle that begins to take over more and more of the open space on her paper. She suddenly gets the idea that she's painting an "abstraction" instead of some recognizable object or scene. No one can check her work and say whether what she has done looks right or good or like anything at all.

Carly imagines Daniel smelling the paint when he comes in and her telling him that her easel is standing by the window in place of the dying ficus tree. She imagines him asking what she has painted, maybe even coming close to stand by her side as she explains. What will she tell him, Carly wonders, and realizes she can tell him anything she likes. Whatever comes to mind is what he'll imagine in his own mind's eye.

But when Daniel gets back, he's in a really bad mood. He slams the door behind him and drops his coat in the middle of the floor. He doesn't even bother to unharness Beacon, who lies down by the coat with his seeing-eye gear still attached to him.

"Hey, how's it going?" Carly asks as she goes over and begins to undo Beacon's harness.

"What are you doing?" Daniel asks.

Even though he can't see, Daniel's sense of hearing is so acute that he recognizes by sound things that go on around him.

"Unharnessing Beacon. He looks uncomfortable."

"He's not uncomfortable, and we're going out again in a little while."

"Aren't we gonna work this afternoon?"

"It's Thursday. I have a session with my shrink," Daniel says.

Carly is surprised she forgot about Daniel's session with Gwen. She's usually very aware of his therapy schedule and follows his moods carefully as he gets ready to leave for a session or returns from one. But since she has been cutting school at Baxter, more and more Carly's days have begun to run together in a blur.

"Oh, right. I forgot. Hey, I brought some stuff over and have been working on a painting."

"Don't you think the smell is pretty strong?"

"I thought you said it'd be OK if—"

"I had no idea how toxic the fumes from the paint would be," Daniel says.

"I didn't realize it would bother you."

"Well, now you know."

"I've got half a sandwich left over from my lunch if you're hungry," Carly tells him. She's trying to be upbeat, but underneath she's feeling deflated. All the good, free feeling from painting an abstraction is gone, and now all Carly feels is fear about what's happening with Daniel.

"Cool. How was *your* day?" Daniel asks as Carly hands him the half sandwich.

"The usual bullshit. My English professor was talking about how Hamlet wants to leave home, to see the world kind of, but his mother wants him to stay home."

When Daniel doesn't say anything, Carly adds, "Kind of reductive, don't you think?"

"Not really. I mean, there's that scene where Hamlet tells his mother, 'I will to Wittenberg,' where he wants to go study, and then she runs her number on him about staying home in boring little Denmark."

"He should've gone," Carly says, laughing it off. "Things might've worked out better if he had."

She gathers up her nerve and decides to ask about the fellowship Daniel's applying for. "I guess you'll be hearing soon about that Fulbright in Germany for next year?"

When Daniel doesn't respond, Carly crosses the room and starts packing up her paints. She's never seen Daniel in such a dark mood before, and she doesn't know what to do to make it better. She's just taking down the easel when he comes up to her from behind and puts his arms around her. His hands find her breasts and inch in between the buttons of her blouse to her bra, and then he works his fingers underneath the fabric until he's touching her bare flesh. "Come to bed," he whispers, and she turns and follows him as he pulls her gently by her hand.

The first part, his wanting her so much he can't wait, is the best part. Carly feels most in control then, because she's what he wants most. When they're doing it, though, she feels kind of out of it and thinks about other things. Sometimes she imagines Lauren with Elliott, and sometimes she pretends she's Naomi doing it with Aaron.

After the first time, Daniel has been using condoms, and Carly looks away as he puts one on before he slides her pants down and climbs on top of her. When he rolls off her a moment later, she feels like the life has just been suctioned out of her. If only he would wrap her in his arms and kiss her instead of turning his head away. If only he'd say, "I love you." The trouble is, it's over so fast, and while it's happening, it feels like Daniel is a million miles away. It actually hurts, the raw, hollow feeling she's left with when it's over.

What Carly can't understand is where the wanting goes when it's happening. She feels it with the touching and kissing that comes before, and then she feels it afterwards, when it's too late. But in the middle all she feels is nervous. Maybe, Carly thinks, the nervous feeling takes the wanting feeling away. She has looked in the books in Gwen's office, the ones on female sexuality, but they never say anything about the stuff that troubles her. Carly wonders if Daniel ever thinks about Gwen when they're doing it and if maybe he sometimes imagines he's doing it with her.

Carly wishes she could slow it all down, replay each time as soon as it's over, like the instant replays of football games. Sometimes when she's by herself, lying on her bed and remembering, Carly can almost feel how good it could be. She tells herself that next time when they're together, she'll feel all the wanting she could ever need.

When Daniel starts pulling up his pants and putting on his shoes, Carly checks her Swatch and realizes he's running late for his session. She senses he's in a mood where anything she says is going to make it worse, so she keeps quiet and watches helplessly as he throws on his jacket and gathers up Beacon's harness.

"See ya tomorrow," is all he says as he heads out the door.

CHAPTER TWENTY-THREE

t feels like the middle of the night when Carly awakens, but when she looks at the clock she sees that it's almost ten o'clock in the morning. How could she have slept through the alarm she always sets on school mornings, she wonders, or did she forget to set it? Sunlight is streaming through the tilted blinds and making the sheet warm to her touch.

A nauseous feeling is the first thing that hits her when she sits up, so Carly lies back down again, but the nausea grows worse. She barely makes it to the toilet in time, but when she actually begins retching, only a thin stream of liquid comes out. Carly has been skipping meals, so it doesn't surprise her that nothing solid comes out. She figures she has some kind of flu.

Gwen has left for the hospital, and Katherine doesn't arrive until the afternoon, so the apartment is quiet. By the time she climbs back in bed, Carly's dizzy and soaked in sweat. She knows she needs to call Ruth at the health food co-op, where she was due in at nine, but she feels too sick to pick up the phone and dial her number.

Lying in bed weak and exhausted, Carly feels like a child again. She remembers her mother rubbing her little girl limbs with a mixture of alcohol and warm water to bring down a fever, then sitting by her side, feeding her soup and watching her crayon between the lines of a coloring book. For a moment, before thoughts break in about cutting school and faking an identity and seeing Daniel on the sly, before she remembers that her life is about keeping secret all the lies, Carly wishes her mother was there to take care of her again.

She closes her eyes and pretends that she's lying on a beach, soaking up the sun, and a feeling of warmth washes over her. A picture from the family album floats across her mind, and she sees herself again as a little girl lying next to her mother on the beach where they went when Carly was a child. Her body is young and round, not long and lean and beautiful like her mother's. But the two of them wear the same red-and-blue-striped bathing suits with bright yellow straps. Carly has heard her father describe how he snapped the shot while she and Gwen slept side by side in the sun, but Carly is sure she remembers when it was taken. The sound of the clicking camera shutter returns with the memory of the roaring surf. She knows she wasn't sleeping, just trying to be exactly like her mother.

Then the nauseous feeling overcomes her again, and Carly bolts out of bed and makes it to the bathroom just in time.

By noon Carly is feeling better. She calls Ruth and tells her she has the flu. She quickly gets dressed in jeans and a sweatshirt so she can leave before Katherine arrives and starts asking questions about why Carly's home in the middle of the day. She tucks her uniform into her knapsack to change into at the end of the day. But just before heading out the door, Carly sees an envelope with Lauren's handwriting on the mail table and stops long enough to read the letter.

Dear Carly,

I hate it here. California is la-la land. All the kids are crazed on Hollywood. At least every other girl in my school thinks she's the next Meg Ryan or Jodie Foster. And the ones who don't, wish they were. No one takes painting or art halfway seriously. Everyone's into drinking juice and body-building. The weather's driving me mad—it's always hot and hazy. Everyone in my class is from what they call in mandatory life science class a "blended family." It sounds like something you make by whipping ice cream and soda together in a blender. BF will probably become the next acronym on the Internet.

In a way, when people do stick together today, it's a miracle. The one thing I'm sure of in life, other than painting, is that I'll never get married. I can't imagine loving any man enough to spend the rest of my life with him. Besides, if you want to be an artist—a real artist, I mean, and not a dilettante who just dabbles in art—you have to give your whole life to it. Every waking hour. Otherwise, life will suck you dry. Look at Tibou, for example. She could've been an artist, I'm absolutely sure of it. She has art in her soul. But it's all gone into omelets and soufflés, and she has nothing left to show for it, and neither does the world.

One good thing is that I got accepted into a figure-drawing class at a private studio where they use nude models. It's the only thing I'm living for in this god-awful outpost of what barely passes for civilization. I've become friends with a very cool French guy named Jean Luc, who paints like a dream. I know what you're thinking, but don't get excited. He's gay and lives with his boyfriend, Olivier, who dances with the Los Angeles Ballet. They have a loft in Chinatown and give great parties.

Tibou and Marc send their love. My father's too busy redesigning the Los Angeles Chamber of Commerce. Did you know that Los Angeles is the fastest-growing county in the U.S. of A.? Be glad you don't live in it. Write soon. I'm starved for news from the homeland.

Hugs, Lauren

Carly usually loves getting letters from Lauren and reads them over and over again. But today feels different, and Lauren's letter seems self-indulgent and overly dramatic. The bit about being an artist and never getting married and putting down Tibou for cooking great omelets sounds so childish. Eager to be on her way, Carly stuffs the letter back in its envelope and puts it away where Gwen won't see it.

When Carly arrives an hour later, Daniel is rummaging nervously around the apartment, looking for his audiobook of *Middlemarch.* When he can't find it, he gets more and more agitated, and Carly asks if she can help.

"I can handle it," Daniel says in a way that lets Carly know she shouldn't interfere. She goes over to Beacon, lying in a patch of sunshine by the window, and plops down by his side.

"Good dog," she tells him soothingly as she strokes his big square head.

"He's resting," Daniel says. "He shouldn't be disturbed."

Carly withdraws her hand and then realizes Daniel can only hear what she says but can't see what she's doing. She puts her hand back on Beacon's head and rubs it some more.

The afternoon is a bust. Daniel's in a bad mood the whole time Carly reads from the Mozart correspondence, and when she tells him it's getting toward the time she has to leave, all he says is, "Yeah, it's getting late. You should go."

Carly gathers up her things and asks him what time he wants her to be there tomorrow.

"We could give it a break for a day or so. I have to work on my paper for Kennedy."

Today is Tuesday, so Carly figures forward and asks, "So how about Thursday? Is that good?"

"I see my shrink on Thursdays. How about we get together again on Friday?"

Carly's heart sinks. That's the longest they will have been apart since her weekend in Vermont with the Lenskys, but she doesn't have a choice, she realizes as she heads for the door.

"Cool," she says, trying to keep her voice light and cheery. "See you Friday."

As she heads out the door, Carly remembers Lauren's letter. Maybe she'll read it again when she gets home, give it another chance. And maybe she'll use the time between now and Friday to write her about what's happening with Daniel. Suddenly, she misses Lauren so much it hurts. She wishes she could just drop in on her the way she used to when the Lenskys lived in the same building instead of all the way across the country.

CHAPTER TWENTY-FOUR

arly startles awake when her alarm goes off at seven on Wednesday morning. As she sits up, she feels the same nauseous, queasy way she felt yesterday morning when she overslept. When the retching ritual repeats itself, Carly realizes that maybe this isn't the flu. Her periods have always been irregular, but even still, it has been quite a while since she last got one. She knows Daniel has been using condoms ever since, but she's quite sure he wasn't using one that first time. That was a month ago, and it was a couple weeks before that, Carly remembers, that she had her last period.

Carly dresses fast and doesn't bother with breakfast. Instead of waiting for the bus, she hails a cab and directs the driver to the West Side. She's wearing her wig, which gives her confidence as she goes to the pharmacy on 113th and Broadway. She spends several minutes browsing before no more people are lined up at the counter. To make it look like she was really searching for something and not just holding back because she was embarrassed, she takes a bottle of shampoo along as she goes up to the counter and asks the pharmacist's assistant for a pregnancy test kit.

A quarter of an hour later, as she steps out of the restroom at the health food co-op, Carly knows she's pregnant. Her first thought is of Tess, who gets pregnant with Alec's baby, Sorrow, who dies at two months old. She wonders if reading *Tess of the d'Urbervilles* was some sort of omen, that Tess's story has somehow infiltrated her life, but before she can develop this thought any further, Ruth tosses an apron at her and directs her to peel the fresh garlic and ginger piled on the butcher-block counter in the middle of the store.

When Carly lets herself into the apartment and sees Gwen sitting in the corner of the living room, pumping one leg nervously over the other, she knows something horrible has happened. It's two thirty on Thursday afternoon, and Gwen should be in her office, seeing a patient.

"Come sit down, Carly," Gwen commands, but before Carly even reaches the living room, Gwen starts interrogating her. "Can you tell me why you've been missing school for the past month?"

Carly remains silent, and Gwen explains that Ms. Harrington called to see how Carly was feeling. The letter about Carly's mononucleosis came up, and that was when Carly's truancy from school was revealed.

"You may as well tell me the whole story, Carly, because whatever it is, you've been put on probation for the rest of the semester until a decision is reached about whether you're to be expelled or to repeat junior year."

The news has a strange effect on Carly. It feels almost like relief.

"I'm not going back to Baxter, and there's nothing to tell," Carly says slowly, watching for Gwen's reaction. "I couldn't take it anymore, so I stopped going. I'm glad I'm on probation, and I hope I get expelled."

"But what have you been doing all this time? How have you been spending the days?"

"Nothing. Hanging out. Walking around the park." A thought crosses Carly's mind that might put a more constructive spin on her situation, and she adds, "Oh, and I've been working in a health food co-op."

Gwen raises an eyebrow and is momentarily wordless before she collects herself and responds, "A health food store? But why?"

"Because I care about being healthy?" Carly ventures, trying to add a touch of humor. "And it's a co-op, not a store."

"I meant what's going on inside you?"

"You mean so you can analyze me, like you analyze your patients? No deal."

"I don't get it, Carly. Where's it coming from, all this anger? Can you tell me—can you at least try to tell me—what it's about?"

"I thought you were supposed to be able to read people's minds and understand their reasons for doing things."

"Nobody can read another person's mind, Carly. People have to talk about their thoughts and feelings for others to understand them."

"Unless they don't want to be understood."

Carly stares Gwen down until she looks away.

"What are we going to do? Have you thought about that?" Gwen asks.

"We? Since when are you involved with my life?"

"I've always been involved with your life, Carly."

"Well, isn't that what mothers are for, to fix things when kids fuck up?"

"Is that what you think, really? That you can do anything you want—fail school, cut class, hang out God knows where and

do God knows what—and then I come along and clean every‑
thing up?"

Carly gets a jolt of energy when she sees her mother losing
control. She feels Gwen's anger seeping through like wet mud
below grass when it rains too hard for the earth to soak up the
overflow. Usually, Carly feels like she's losing with her mother,
but right now, when she sees how upset her mother is, she feels
like she's winning.

"I don't think anything," Carly screams, "and I could care
less about going to a shithole place like Baxter! Who the fuck
is Willoughby Harrington, and what the fuck has she done
to deserve playing God with other people's lives? I hope I get
kicked out."

"Well, if you do get expelled, Willoughby Harrington will be
giving up the role of 'playing God' with your life, and you'll have
to take responsibility for what comes next, Carly."

The doorbell rings, and Gwen stands up. "We have to con‑
tinue this later, Carly."

"Your next patient is here, Dr. Klein. Do you get off on the
dog too? Or is it just the blind guy that turns you on?"

Before Gwen has a chance to answer, Carly has left the room.

CHAPTER TWENTY-FIVE

"Hi there," Carly says as Daniel lets her into his apartment. "How's it going?"

"Great," Daniel says, but Carly can tell he's not in a good mood.

"Any luck finding the *Middlemarch* tape?"

"No problem," Daniel says, but Carly's not sure if that means the problem is solved because he found it, or it's not a problem that it's still lost.

"We can start right in on Mozart's correspondence if you want," Carly offers, trying to be helpful, and heads over to the shelf where she left the book the last time she read for Daniel.

"How about we read my mail first today?"

Carly changes direction and goes over to the table by the door, where a hefty stack of letters and papers has been accumulating.

"Any special order?" she asks as she settles down on the floor with the pile in her lap.

"Do you see anything with Fulbright in the return address?"

Carly shuffles through the bundle and singles something out. "Bingo! Shall I open it?"

"Go for it!"

Carly carefully opens the envelope and pulls out a thick sheet of stationery with *Fulbright Scholar Program* on the letterhead. She takes a deep breath and begins to read, "'Dear Mr. Strauss, We are pleased to inform you that the Fulbright Committee—'"

"Whoopee! I made it!" Daniel shouts before Carly can read any further.

When Carly pauses, Daniel stops shouting and demands, "Well, what are you waiting for? Read the rest."

"'We are pleased to inform you that the Fulbright Committee has awarded you a one-year fellowship to pursue the study of music as outlined in your application proposal, in Munich, Germany, for the academic year 1991–1992.'"

Daniel walks over to the window and starts fingering the cord on the venetian blind, wrapping it around and around his hand. The meaning of this news begins to sink in, and Carly realizes that Daniel will really be going to Germany next year and leaving her behind. A feeling of desperation wells up inside her, and when he doesn't say anything, Carly gets an idea.

"I should finish reading the letter. I didn't read it all." She stares at the page as she recites: "'This fellowship has a provision for bringing an assistant with you.'"

Carly looks over at Daniel to see his reaction, but he's not smiling.

"Oh, and it says Beacon can come too."

"That's not funny," Daniel snaps.

"Sorry," Carly says.

"You have to finish college, Serena."

Carly's voice comes out small and high when she says, "People sometimes take a year off."

"For Chrissake, Serena. You have to do your own thing."

Carly thinks of Tess and how her world collapses when

Angel goes off to Brazil without her. In the background she hears Daniel saying, "I know you'd like to come to Germany with me, Serena, but the Fulbright's my job, and your job is to finish college."

"Don't you think it's my job to decide what I should do with my life?"

Carly is fighting back tears that in another moment she won't be able to hold in any longer.

"It's my fellowship, Serena. You decide about your life, and I decide about mine."

"I get it." Carly is crying now. "You don't need me anymore, now that you got the Fulbright."

Carly can barely see through the blur of tears as she begins to gather up her belongings. Daniel heads toward her, but she moves so fast he has trouble locating her.

"Hey, slow down, Serena. Can't we talk about it?"

"There's nothing to talk about."

Carly throws the letters and papers on the table by the door, and as the pile splays out she notices a page with an A on it. She looks closer and sees the title, "*Tess of the d'Urbervilles*: Trial and Temptation in the Chase," followed by Daniel's name. To make sure of what she already knows, Carly thumbs through the stapled pages and recognizes her own typed text.

"You submitted my paper for Kennedy's course?"

Daniel doesn't say anything, and Carly repeats, "I asked you, Daniel, did you hand in my paper?"

"Oh, right, yeah. I was gonna tell you. Kennedy loved it. You got an A."

"*I* didn't get an A. *You* got an A on *my* paper."

"Hey, calm down. I couldn't find my copy of *Middlemarch* in time."

"You didn't even like my interpretation," Carly says.

"That's not true. I thought what you wrote was right on the money."

"You stole my paper!"

"It's not stealing. I was right that Kennedy would love it. I told you he'd give you an A on it."

Carly's shaking now. She feels like something is disintegrating inside her, like paper being torn to pieces in a shredder. Outside Daniel's window, night is falling. The sky has turned the black and blue of bruises shot with patches of tender pinky orange.

"Hey, look," Daniel says, sounding impatient and condescending, as though Carly's just a kid. "You're just upset about the Fulbright thing and Germany. I know you're disappointed we won't be together, and you're taking it out on the paper."

Carly stuffs her jacket into her knapsack and races for the door.

"You think you're such a liberated person with all that bullshit about being a feminist even though you're a guy, but you're no better than all the other guys who use women for sex and for—and for . . . stealing their work."

Carly flings the door open and is about to run out when she thinks of one more thing she wants to say.

"And just 'cause you're blind, you know, that doesn't make you better than other people. It doesn't mean that when you lie and cheat, you're not as much of a bastard as someone who can see."

Daniel stands very still, his back up against the far wall of the apartment. As soon as she hurls the angry words his way, Carly's sorry. Now there's nothing left to do but run away.

CHAPTER
TWENTY-SIX

Katherine is gone for the day when Carly gets home, and according to the note on the refrigerator door, Gwen is in a meeting and won't be home for another hour. Carly's grounded except for when she's working at the health food co-op, which gives her enough flexibility to come and go pretty much as she chooses, except in the evenings, when she's not allowed to go out. The apartment is dark, but Carly doesn't bother turning on lights as she heads upstairs.

As though gazing through the distancing lens of a telescope, she sees the apartment and all of its contents like the miniaturized version of childhood in a dollhouse display. A chasm has opened up between the now that she's living and her earlier life, which seems incredibly far away, as though Carly has crossed some invisible barrier of time and space and is looking back on another civilization.

She dumps her knapsack on her bed and feels like an intruder as she heads for Gwen's office. When she places her hand on the doorknob, she thinks of wiping it with a cloth to remove her handprint.

Once inside, Carly works fast. She goes straight to the

cabinet where Gwen stores the notebooks and rifles through them until she finds Daniel's. With her heart pounding so hard that her chest actually aches, Carly opens to the latest entry and frantically scans the page. With blood pounding through her head and her breath catching in her throat, it feels as though she's beginning to suffocate.

Carly races through paragraphs filled with observations on Daniel's concerns about his work, his application for a Fulbright scholarship, his anxiety about next year and the future in general.

Tears spring into pools at the lower edge of Carly's eyes. She has to hold still, because if she tilts her head down or blinks, they'll spill over onto the page, soaking into the paper and making the words blur and run.

Then, toward the bottom of the page, Carly suddenly sees the initial S. She follows the notes to where Gwen has written, *D. feeling trapped. Sexual relations with S. strained by lack of response. D. looking for way out.*

Before the tears that have pooled in her eyes have a chance to overflow onto the page, Carly closes the notebook. She carefully returns it to the correct place in the filing cabinet, where Gwen stores the notebooks alphabetically by patients' names, and closes the office door behind her as she leaves.

Back in her own room, Carly goes over to the bed and pulls down the covers. From her closet she pulls out a spare comforter and bunches it up on the bottom sheet before pulling the covers back up. She puts her gray stuffed squirrel on a pile of pillows and stands back by the door to assess the overall effect. It does look like someone's under the covers in the bed, Carly thinks. And Gwen won't bother coming in any farther if the lights are out and she thinks Carly's asleep for the night. Carly checks around her room and turns off the light before closing the door behind her.

Out in the hall, Carly presses the button for the elevator and rides it down to the lobby. It's already eight thirty, and Gwen may be coming home. If she meets her mother on her way out, Carly thinks, she'll surely die. She exits the building just as a cab pulls up in front. As she runs down the block, Carly makes out the profile of her mother leaning forward to pay the driver.

Once she's safely out of sight of her building, breathing hard from running to the bus stop on Madison Avenue, Carly realizes she didn't take her knapsack or a wallet, and she doesn't have her wig. She roots around in her clothing, and all she finds is an old library card with her name and a picture that was taken at least two years ago and a few coins in her coat and pants pockets. She won't be able to take the bus, because she doesn't have any tokens, and she doesn't have enough money for a cab. She decides she'll walk there.

As she sets out on foot for Central Park, Carly forces herself to stop thinking of what she'll say when she gets to Daniel's place. Something will come to her. She'll just take it one step at a time.

When she reaches Daniel's building, Carly's not sure what she came here to say. She needs to let Daniel know that she's sorry about the horrible things she said earlier in the day, about the insults she hurled at him. She needs to tell him she's pregnant with his baby and that she still wants to be with him. She needs to find out if this will change his mind about going to Germany and leaving her behind.

When she gets to his apartment and rings the bell, it takes a few minutes for him to open the door. He doesn't invite her in when she tells him, "It's me, Serena." He just stands there waiting for her to explain why she has come.

"I have to talk to you, Daniel. I have something important to tell you."

"You told me everything I need to know before. You can go away now."

"But you don't know that I'm pregnant, that I'm having your baby."

During the pause when Daniel doesn't say anything, Carly says a silent prayer. *Please let him love me and our baby.* But when he does answer, it's not what Carly hoped for.

"You're just a sophomore, Serena, and you're too young to have anyone's baby."

"It's not anyone's baby."

Carly's voice is louder than she intended, and Daniel pulls her out of the hall and into the apartment, closing the door behind her as she screams, "It's your baby, Daniel, and it's your fault for not using protection the first time!"

"Most girls use their own protection—pills or a diaphragm. How was I to know you were a virgin? You never told me before it was too late."

"You're saying it's my fault?"

Carly meant for this to be different, for her to be calm and for Daniel to be gentle, but it's not happening like that, and she's losing control again, just like before.

"It's not your fault, Serena. It's something that happens. You can do something about this. It can be taken care of."

"You mean abortion? You're saying I should have an abortion because you didn't use protection and it's my fault 'cause it was my first time?"

"I'm saying that this kind of thing happens, and it doesn't have to be the end of the world."

"You mean your world!" Carly's screaming and sobbing at the same time now. "It doesn't have to be the end of your world because it's not your problem or your responsibility."

Her tears back up into her throat, and she begins to choke

and cough. When Daniel offers her a glass of water, Carly nods her head and then remembers Daniel can't see her signaling yes. She knows she's completely invisible to him. Not only can't he see the tears streaming down her face, he can't see or feel her pain either.

"Yes," she whispers. "I'd like some water."

It takes a few moments for Daniel to cross the room, fill a glass with water, and return. Beacon follows him with his eyes from where he lies with his head on his crossed paws.

In the meantime, Carly sees her *Tess* paper on the table by the door in the same place she left it a few hours ago. She goes over, picks it up, and tears off the cover page with the A and her title with Daniel's name below it. She balls it up and throws it on the floor. She looks around and finds a pen lying on the table, scribbles CARLY KLEIN in big block print at the top of the first page, and then folds the stapled essay in half and tucks it in her pocket.

"Thank you," Carly says as Daniel hands her the glass. She gulps down a couple swallows and pours the rest of the water on the floor where the balled-up title page has landed by Daniel's feet.

"Here," she tells him, and hands back the glass.

"Thanks," Daniel says.

"For nothing," Carly tells him, and heads out the door.

Down on the street, Carly doesn't know what to do and where to go. If only Lauren lived somewhere close by, she'd go to her now and tell her the whole story of what has happened to her life. She thinks of going to her father's apartment, ringing the bell and appearing at his door, but Edwin might be there. They might be having a date or whatever they do when they're in their own life together.

When Carly gets to Broadway, she sees the phone booth where she first called Daniel, and she decides to call her father. If he picks up and sounds glad to hear from her, she'll ask if she can come over. Then maybe she can even sleep on his couch. Carly puts a quarter in the slot and dials her dad's number. Joel picks up and answers with his usual abbreviated version of "Hello," which comes out sounding more like "'Lo." Carly feels reassured when she hears his voice and the familiar greeting, but then just as she's about to say something, she hears another voice in the background, a man's, calling, "Phone's ringing. Can you get it, Joel?" Carly recognizes Edwin's voice and quickly slams the receiver back down on the hook.

As she leaves the phone booth, a wet drop falls on Carly's face. She stands unmoving on the street corner, and the rain makes a loud, whistling sound as it pours down from above.

Just then Carly thinks of Ruth, who lives upstairs from the health food co-op on 113th and Broadway. The rain begins to soak through Carly's sweater, and a chill takes hold of her whole body.

It's late and dark when Carly arrives. Right next door to the co-op, which is locked for the night, is the entryway to the upstairs apartments. Carly enters and presses the button by Ruth Waddell's name on the keypad. It didn't occur to Carly that Ruth might not be home, but when no one answers, she rings again and then a third time before she realizes Ruth isn't there.

Dizzy and weak, Carly leans up against the wall. At least the narrow entryway provides shelter from the rain that's pouring down outside. Shaking with cold, she feels her knees buckle under her as she slides down to the floor.

She has no idea what time it is and no idea how long she has been there when a woman with a dog comes down from upstairs and finds her huddled there.

"What are you doing?" the woman says as Carly struggles through a confusion of dreams and sensations to become conscious again.

She must have fallen asleep, she realizes. She has a splitting headache, and when she tries to get up, her legs give out again, and she slides back down to the floor.

"Are you sick?" the woman asks. "Shall I call an ambulance?"

Carly startles at the suggestion of an ambulance. Pressing her hands against the wall to steady herself, she manages to summon enough strength to pull herself to her feet.

"I'm OK," she tells the woman, whose little dog is barking and jumping up and down by the door. "I was just keeping out of the rain."

"You look like you need help," the woman says. "I can make a call for you if you like."

"No, that's OK," Carly says, and pushes past her and the barking dog out onto the street.

It's raining so hard, and Carly's so weak and dizzy, she can't tell which direction she's going as she hugs close to the building to steady herself. She's stumbling along the sidewalk when the woman calls back after her: "Wait, you need help."

At the corner of 116th Street and Broadway, Carly recognizes the place where the old Black man with the xylophone sets up his workstation. But he has packed up and left for wherever it is he goes when the day is done. The island dividing the north- and southbound sides of Broadway is empty now. Just some old newspapers and food wrappers and the old Black man's plaid blanket remain. He's probably coming back for it in the morning, Carly figures, but in the meantime, she's freezing and exhausted, and even though the blanket is soaking wet, she decides to wrap it around her for a few minutes while she figures out where she should go next.

When Carly awakens, she's trembling with cold. Her teeth are chattering so violently it feels like she could actually break them. Her body is shaking so hard that she's afraid she's going to fall off the narrow seat. She rolls over and grabs the slats on the back of the bench with both hands and clenches as hard as she can before passing out.

CHAPTER
TWENTY-SEVEN

G wen is sleeping across the room in a chair by the window when Carly awakens. She slowly becomes aware of where she is and why. She sees on the clock by her bedside that it's two thirty in the afternoon. She realizes she has been sleeping since early that morning when she first regained consciousness and saw she was being brought by ambulance to the emergency room at Mount Sinai Hospital.

Carly watches Gwen as she sleeps. It hurts her to see her mother, who always dresses in nice clothes when she works at the hospital, in sweats and running shoes with messy hair that needs brushing. The sweatshirt and sweatpants she's wearing don't even match.

When a nurse comes in and tells Carly she's here to take her vitals, Gwen startles awake. She jumps up and starts toward Carly's bed, but when she sees her sitting up and talking to the nurse, Gwen backs off and sits back down again while the nurse takes Carly's temperature and blood pressure and checks the IV tube that's connected to her left hand.

"How long till they take this thing out?" Carly asks the nurse.

"When the doctor comes by later, you can ask him," the nurse tells her. "The more liquids you get down by mouth, the sooner that will happen."

Carly looks around and finds a cup filled with water by her bedside and gulps down its contents.

"Atta girl," the nurse says as she refills the cup from a plastic pitcher. "A few more of those, and you'll be off IV in no time. Anything else for now before I leave?"

A memory of the filthy bench on Broadway where she collapsed floods back, and Carly asks, "When can I take a shower?"

"I'll put in for an aide to help with that."

"I don't need help to shower."

"You do to get untangled from that," the nurse says, pointing at Carly's IV tube.

"I can't just pull it out?"

"Hang in there, hon. You're gonna be feeling much better as soon as you get some liquids going."

"A shower's liquid," Carly says, smiling for the first time.

"I'll see if I can rustle up an aide as soon as possible," the nurse tells her before leaving the room.

Carly feels guilty to be ignoring her mother, who has retreated in silence to her chair across the room. "How'd you find out I was here, Mom?"

"From the library card that was in your jacket pocket. The hospital called me when they figured out who you were."

"You look exhausted," Carly tells her.

"How are *you* feeling?" Gwen asks, crossing the room to Carly's bedside.

"Like shit," Carly tells her.

"May I sit down?" Gwen asks, pointing at the bed.

"If you want," Carly says, nervous about what's coming next.

"I want."

They sit without speaking for the next few moments until Carly breaks the silence.

"I know you hate me for what I did."

"I don't hate you at all. I hate myself for what I didn't do."

Gwen's eyes have deep hollows below them, and she looks sadder and more defeated than Carly has ever seen her look.

"What didn't you do?" Carly asks in a weak voice.

"I didn't take care of my own little girl."

Gwen's eyes fill up with tears that spill over and run down her cheeks. Carly swallows hard and looks away. When she looks back, Gwen is just sitting there forlorn, not wiping away the tears. Carly plucks a tissue from the box on her bed stand and dabs Gwen's cheeks. Gwen brings Carly's hand with the tissue to her mouth and gently kisses it.

"I should be taking care of you, wiping up your tears," Gwen tells Carly.

"I don't have any more tears," Carly says, and begins to cry.

"You've been very brave and very grown-up," Gwen says gently. "It's time for you to be my little girl again."

When her mother takes her in her arms, Carly lays her head on Gwen's shoulder and sobs.

An aide knocks on the door and comes in and introduces herself.

"Hi, Carly. I'm Maria, and I'm here to help you with shower."

Carly tenses at first, embarrassed to be seen sobbing on her mother's shoulder. She quickly pulls away and collects herself. "Great. Can you untangle me from all these tubes and wires?"

"That's my job," Maria says brightly, and sets about disconnecting the IV.

"Ouch, that hurts," Carly says as Maria pulls the tube from the little port where it's connected to her hand.

"I know, I know. I try to make less painful when I connect later."

"Can't you just skip that part?" Carly asks.

"I know, I know. You no like IV tube. No one like IV tube."

Carly comes out of the shower a few minutes later in a fresh hospital gown and gets settled back in bed with the IV reconnected. Gwen is back sitting in the chair by the window with a stapled paper in her lap.

"I hope you don't mind that I read your paper on *Tess of the d'Urbervilles*. It was in your jacket pocket."

"I guess you're wondering what that's all about since I wasn't going to school anymore, at least not to Baxter."

"I'm wondering about a lot of things that I've missed," Gwen says as she gets up and sits back down on the edge of the bed.

"Aren't you gonna start asking questions?"

Gwen gently covers Carly's hand with the IV tube with her own. "When you're ready to let me in on what you want to tell me, I'll be here."

Carly's silent for a while, thinking over how different her mom seems from the mom from before all this happened.

"Don't you have to do stuff at the hospital and see patients?"

"I've canceled my patients, and right now being with you is what I have to do at the hospital."

"I'm pregnant. And he wants me to have an abortion."

Gwen nods her head very slowly. "You had a miscarriage, Carly, and so the pregnancy's over now."

"Oh my God. How . . . how did that happen? How do you know?"

"You were suffering from overexposure, malnutrition, and an electrolyte imbalance, all of which contributed to weakening your overall condition. Your body was fighting back, and this was . . . this was its way of responding."

The thought of Tibou's baby being stillborn crosses Carly's mind, and she shudders and hugs her arms around herself.

"Does that mean I can never get pregnant again, that I can't have another baby?"

"Oh no, no, not at all. A miscarriage means that just this pregnancy has ended. Someday, when you're older and much more ready for it, you'll become pregnant and have a fine baby."

"I want lots of them, not just one," Carly says defiantly.

"There will be time for babies. Lots of time."

"Don't you want to know how I got pregnant? I mean, who it was?"

"I want to know everything you want to share with me." Gwen's voice cracks as she adds, "I know this may be hard for you to believe, since I obviously haven't been there for you for quite some time, but I am now."

"I've been really bad and done some really awful things."

"We've all done bad things, Carly. That doesn't make us bad people."

Carly looks down as she says very quietly, "It was your patient Daniel. I lied and faked an identity . . ."

Gwen's eyes open wide and her body stiffens. She takes her hand from Carly's and covers her mouth.

"Serena . . . You're Daniel's Serena . . ."

Carly nods her head but doesn't say anything. Tears run down her cheeks, and Gwen just shakes her head back and forth with shock and disbelief.

"I followed him to campus and answered an ad for a reader that he posted on a bulletin board. I began reading for him—the letters from Mozart and his family—and then I started hanging out with him and going to class. That's why I wrote the paper on Tess, but I couldn't hand it in because I wasn't actually taking the course. Then Daniel stole it and submitted it to the course—and got an A on it. When I found out and got angry at him for stealing it, we had a big fight and broke up. I left, and it was raining and I had no place to go because I couldn't come home because I knew you'd be furious with me for breaking curfew after I was already on probation, and I . . . and I was at the end of my rope and didn't know what to do . . ." Carly starts sobbing again, harder than before. "I wanted to die. I just wanted to die and make everything go away and be over with. I guess I almost got my way." Carly pauses and then adds, "I made my baby go away."

"You were just a few weeks pregnant, Carly. That's not a baby yet."

"Embryos grow into babies, and I killed mine."

"You didn't kill anything, Carly. You were weak and debilitated, and you suffered emotional and physical trauma that induced a miscarriage."

"Are you sure I can have another baby? Are you sure?"

"Yes, I'm sure, Carly. That you became pregnant actually establishes your fertility." Gwen pauses and then makes a decision. "Which means that in the future you'll need to take proper precautions to protect yourself."

"You mean get birth control?"

"Exactly."

"Daniel said it was my fault that I didn't use any, at least the first time."

"That's all it takes." Gwen smiles to show she's not judging.

That lightens up her words enough for Carly to say, "Apparently."

"Tess learned the hard way too," Gwen says gently, rubbing her hand lightly over Carly's while avoiding the IV tube.

"What did you think of my paper?"

"I thought it was extraordinary, the best I've read from you."

"I guess going to college made me a better student." Given

the irony, Carly forgets her misery and feels proud of herself.

"I think so," Gwen muses. "It's an interesting form of rebellion you chose: cutting high school so you could go to college."

"I really liked it. I sat in on really cool classes and learned lots of stuff that interested me a whole lot more than what was going on at Baxter."

"Well, there are lots of different kinds of high schools, and I'm sure that if we look carefully, we can find one that fits your needs."

"You mean, you're not sorry I got put on probation and might get kicked out of Baxter?"

"I'm sorry that I missed so many signals, Carly, and that I didn't understand how unhappy you were."

Suddenly, Carly wants to confess everything, wipe the slate clean so she can start all over again. "There's something else you need to know, something else I did that will definitely make you mad."

"It's possible for a person to be angry and to forgive."

"But you don't know what you have to forgive me for yet."

"I'll try my best to be forgiving when I do know what that is."

"It's not gonna be easy."

"None of this is easy, Carly, but we're doing what we need to do, which is to go through it so we can come out on the other side."

"I read your notebooks, the ones you keep about patients . . ."

Gwen doesn't answer for the longest time, and Carly gets the feeling she has really blown it now. This has pushed her mother over the top, and there will be no coming back from this.

"I guess there's some stuff that's so bad it can't be forgiven."

"It never occurred to me to lock them up, as I should have," Gwen says, almost to herself.

"So I couldn't get to them?"

"So they were protected as confidential material, which

is what they should have been. It's my fault that I didn't take proper precaution."

"Kind of like not using birth control?"

"You could say that," Gwen answers.

"You should have protected your files from a thief and a liar like me."

"From a naturally curious child of a parent who wasn't paying proper attention. I fell down on my professional as well as my parental responsibility by leaving those files unsecured."

"So you're saying I didn't do anything wrong?"

"I'm saying that what you did do, which was wrong, was done for reasons that explain why you were able to get away with doing it. I should have been more attentive, both to you and to my work. As for what you did, that remains your responsibility. We're both human and fallible, Carly, and we both made mistakes. We both have work to do."

"What's gonna happen now with Daniel? Is he still gonna be your patient?"

"What happens with our remaining time working together is protected by doctor-patient confidentiality."

"Are there parent-child confidentiality rules too?"

"Let's put some in place right away, Carly. Whatever you and I talk about stays strictly between ourselves. Deal?"

"Is it OK if I tell you stuff about Daniel that I don't like?"

"Of course. And every single thing you share will stay between us. Do we have a deal?"

"Deal," Carly says with conviction, and then adds in a quiet voice that wobbles a little, "I love you, Mom."

"I love you too, Carly, more than I've let you know," Gwen tells her, and begins to cry again.

CHAPTER TWENTY-EIGHT

G wen is reading on the sofa when Carly, still in pajamas, comes down from her bedroom at noon on Saturday.

"I need to do something that you're not gonna like, Mom. I feel I have to come clean, and I know that if I do this, I could cause more damage than I've already caused."

Gwen closes her book and sits up. "Tell me what you feel you need to do, Carly, and then we'll talk about consequences."

Gwen has lightened up her work schedule, and for the time being has been seeing patients at her office at the hospital rather than at home. She says it's so she can spend more "unstructured" time—Gwen's term—around the house, being available to watch movies and to listen to music and just hang out and talk with Carly.

But Carly knows this also has to do with her reading her mother's session notes and, most of all, with what happened with Daniel. Now Gwen keeps her office locked when she's not at home, and since patients haven't been coming to the apartment, Carly isn't thinking about them so much anymore. Except for Daniel, of course. She still thinks about him all the time.

Carly would give anything if she could take it all back, following him to Columbia and answering his reader notice, the fake name and identity, the lies and deceit. Even though Daniel treated her badly at the end, she realizes she also treated him badly by using him for her own selfish needs. She hates herself for taking advantage of a disadvantaged person and feels guilty that she went and did the thing she least meant to do.

It's over now, and Carly accepts that she can't change what was. But she has an unanswered question that she can't just put away. It keeps gnawing at her. She needs to know if Daniel knows who she really is. She wants to know if Gwen told him and how he reacted, if she did. But Gwen has made it clear that what goes on between her and Daniel is protected by the rules of doctor-patient confidentiality.

Carly still blames Daniel for stealing her paper and lying and cheating by submitting it to Kennedy under his own name. But she also blames herself for faking her identity and lying to Daniel about who she was when she worked herself into his life. She knows that if he hadn't been blind, she never could have gotten away with what she did. So in a way, they're even. He stole her paper, but only after she stole the truth from their relationship.

What was her purpose, Carly wonders now that she looks back on the mess she made not only of her own life but of her mother's life too? Of course, Carly never imagined all these complications when she came up with the crazy idea of following Daniel and becoming his reader and then his girlfriend and all the rest that happened. Lauren didn't imagine them either, or she never would have prodded Carly into calling Daniel and all the rest. Carly paces back and forth across the room as she speaks.

"I need to tell Daniel who I am and what I did and why I did it. I need to stop living that lie, but in order to make it end, I have to admit that it happened, and I have to explain it."

"And when you 'come clean' and admit what you did and who you really are, how will you explain why you did it? Have you figured that out for yourself yet?"

"I think I have an idea of what I was doing, or trying to do, and even though it's fucked up and makes no sense, I think my faking who I was had to do with my not feeling real in my own self and in my own life."

These feelings are so fresh and raw and have been held in check for so long that Carly can barely stop the rush of emotion that's coming to the surface. When she pauses to catch her breath, Gwen reaches out a hand and pats the sofa next to her.

"It's not fucked up, and it makes a lot of sense. Come sit down."

Carly is still too pent up to sit and continues pacing as she goes on.

"I never got to choose who I was. Instead, I got told who I was by you, and you didn't really have a clue about who I was because you never paid any attention to me and what I was made of inside. You just figured I was like you, that I wanted what you wanted and needed the same things you needed."

Carly pauses as a memory comes to her.

"I never told you that one day last summer after working on the children's floor, I saw you giving a paper at Mount Sinai."

"Tell me now," Gwen says gently.

"You were talking about an 'invisible light' that's inside everyone as they're growing up. You said it's the parents' job to see that light and to let their child use it to figure out who she is."

"I remember giving that paper. It was quite a while ago. I never knew you heard it."

"That's the only part I heard, but I guess it made a big impression 'cause I've never forgotten it. It's a metaphor, isn't it, seeing the 'invisible light'?"

"That's true. It's a metaphor for perception in general. We use the expression 'to see the light,' by which we mean 'to understand.'"

Carly takes a seat in a chair across from Gwen as she listens to what she's saying.

"I think you must have felt that even though I talked about the 'invisible light' that illuminates every child, I missed seeing that light when it came to you."

"When you chose a place like Baxter to send me to, that was what you needed when you were young. That was your 'light,' to go to a girls school so you could get out from under the influence of your father and your brothers. But I didn't have any brothers and my father was never around, and when he was, he could have cared less about dominating me. He left that to you while he was busy faking his identity and lying to you and me about who he really was."

Carly is realizing the truth as it comes off her tongue.

"Dad even fooled you for all those years when the two of you were acting like normal married people raising a child in a normal home. But your marriage was a lie, and we weren't a normal family at all. And the worst part is that even though I always felt it, even though I always knew something was wrong and that I wasn't like anyone else, I thought it was just me until I realized it was really about us. Our family was what was different because we weren't really a family at all."

When Carly looks up, she expects to see her mother cowering from her assault, but instead Gwen is nodding her head.

"You look like you approve of all these horrible things I'm accusing you and Dad of."

"I approve of your honesty in saying how you really feel, Carly."

Instead of blame or punishment, Gwen's words feel like what Katherine calls "absolution." Carly remembers Katherine explaining, *You tell the priest what you've done and what's in your heart, and he forgives you and absolves you of sin.*

"You've figured out a lot of things, I see," Gwen says, "and you feel the need to share some of these things not only with me but with Daniel?"

"I think I owe him an explanation. It was a lie, the whole relationship, and it doesn't seem fair that only I know that. He still thinks—unless you told him—I was the person I pretended to be. It's like what Dad did to you . . . to us."

"And what if you did let Daniel know? How would that change things?"

"I . . . I don't know how that would change things for Daniel, but I think it would set things right for me."

"A kind of closure, maybe? A sense of completion?"

"Yeah, something like that. So I could move on and stop thinking about him and feeling awful all the time."

"And how do you imagine going about what you feel you need to do?"

"I think I need to see him one more time. I will tell him my side of the story and what I did and why I'm sorry and how I feel that some of the problems were because of me."

Carly stops talking and gets up and begins pacing again.

"I know I wasn't ready for the sex. I know I wasn't very good at it and that he didn't find me . . ." Carly pauses and makes air quotes. "He didn't find me 'responsive.'"

"It's OK to talk about these things," Gwen says quietly.

"I read it in the notes," Carly says, and begins to cry. "Like a thief, I snuck into your office even after I started being with Daniel and read what he said about me in your notebook. How shitty was that? I not only broke into your confidential files, I went behind Daniel's back and spied on his private therapy. How fucked up is that?"

"It's part of an important story, Carly: the story of your life. you wrote a very important chapter in that life that—"

"Kind of like *Tess*," Carly interrupts.

"Except that Hardy wrote Tess's story. You're writing your own story, and because you're the author, you get to decide what happens next."

Carly sucks up her tears and wipes her nose on the sleeve of her shirt. "Gross," she says as Gwen gets up and hands her a tissue.

"So you're saying it's OK if I go talk to Daniel one more time?" Carly asks once she has blown her nose.

Gwen doesn't answer, and Carly says, "I guess you don't think that's such a good idea."

"Daniel has left New York."

"But it's the middle of the term. He can't have left! He hasn't finished his paper on Mozart."

Carly feels a stab of pain when she hears that Daniel is gone. Even though she hasn't seen him for a few weeks—since that awful night when she went for the last time to his apartment— she has thought of him often and always imagined he was right across town, close enough to reach if she needed to see him.

"I wouldn't have mentioned this, except to spare you further disappointment if you were to go back to his apartment to find him."

"Did Daniel let you know he was leaving, or did he just not show up? I can't believe he'd just drop out of senior year."

"You know I'm not at liberty to discuss what happened with a patient."

"I read your notes when he got angry in his session with you, and you thought he was scared about finishing college and therapy and going away."

Gwen's eyes open wide again in startled recognition, the way they did when Carly told her for the first time about sneaking into her office and reading the notes.

"I know I shouldn't know that," Carly tells her.

"But you do know it, and that's the reality we have to deal with."

Carly thinks Gwen looks sad and defeated, as though she's trapped in a corner by what Carly has done.

"Don't be sad, Mom," Carly says, "it's my fault that all this happened. Daniel wouldn't have left and quit therapy if he wasn't so angry with what was happening with me."

Gwen shakes her head. "Listen to me very carefully, Carly. I want you to understand that you are in no way to blame for Daniel's decision to leave."

"It's like he was breaking up with both of us, pushing us both away."

When Gwen is silent for a while, Carly says, "Maybe it's for the best. Maybe he doesn't have to know who I was after all. I didn't even know who I was."

Gwen mulls this over before she says, "That's another way of thinking about it."

"Does that mean you haven't told him about me?" Carly asks.

"I promised you that I would protect our mother-daughter confidentiality."

"Do you think we could make this our own secret and that maybe Daniel never needs to know?"

"I think that's your choice to make, Carly."

When Carly crosses the room and sits down on the sofa, Gwen moves beside her and takes her hand.

"Thank you, Mom. That's what I needed to hear. I think I'd like to keep this just between you and me."

"I also want to say one more thing, Carly. You're just at the very beginning of becoming a woman. Each relationship you'll have will be different, and when you fall in love at the right time with the right person, the two of you will come together in ways that were not available to you in the relationship with Daniel."

Carly knows her mother's talking about sex and saying that it can be different, that it doesn't have to be the way it was with Daniel. Carly wonders if the same goes for her mother, that whatever it was like with Joel doesn't mean it can't be better with someone else. This isn't the right time to work these thoughts out, but Carly has the feeling she'll come back to them later when she's alone so she can try them out on herself and imagine what falling in love with the right person will be like someday.

"I like that you're not in a rush all the time anymore," Carly tells her mother as they lie foot-to-foot on the living room sofa, watching replays of *Little House on the Prairie* and sharing a bowl of popcorn. Carly's still in the same pajamas, and Gwen has changed into her own.

"Me too," Gwen says, and leans forward to help herself to another handful of popcorn as the second episode they're watching ends.

"Are you too tired," Gwen asks, "or could you watch one more?"

"I'm fine," Carly says, and clicks the remote to start another episode.

Even though they're becoming friends, Carly and Gwen are still mother and daughter, and there are still rough, raw spaces between them and tricky places where they fall into sinkholes and can't reach one another. But they're developing a kind of synchrony they never had before. Lately, they've even been building something that feels like trust.

"It was fun having a pajama party with you," Gwen tells

Carly when they finally turn off the television and head up to bed. "I never did that when I was young."

"How come?"

"My parents were very strict and didn't allow sleepovers. When I was eleven, my mom died, and I guess my brothers and I had to grow up fast."

Carly feels herself welling up with questions. There's so much more she wants to know about what it was like for Gwen to be young and have siblings and what it felt like to have your mother die when you were still a child. But it's very late and Gwen is hugging her good night at the top of the stairs. The evening they've spent feels good and complete the way it is.

CHAPTER
TWENTY-NINE

When Carly arrives at her father's apartment, Edwin lets her in.

"Joel's not home yet, so you get me for a while."

Carly's taken aback. She's not sure she wants to be alone with Edwin, and a flash of anger passes through her that her father let this happen.

Edwin opens the door extra wide, holds out his arm with a flourish, and bows his head slightly. "Please," he says, showing her the way, as though he's a butler welcoming a guest at a fancy estate. "Would you like something cold to drink? There's some iced tea or sparkling water."

"I'm OK," Carly says, and brushes by him. "I mean, about a drink."

She hangs her jacket over the back of one of the Biedermeier chairs and adds as an afterthought, "There's not much else about me that's OK."

"You've had a hard run," Edwin says, and refills his glass with iced tea from a pitcher with slices of lemon floating in it. "Sure you won't have a glass? Hydration and all that?"

Carly laughs and changes her mind. "I'll take a little. Thanks."

"It kind of levels the playing field," Edwin says.

"Iced tea?" Carly asks.

"I mean, what's going on with you and Joel."

Carly takes the glass from Edwin, flops down on the sofa across the room, and puts her feet up on the oval cocktail table with the sculpted snake with brass balls for eyes wrapped around one of the legs. It's cool the way Edwin refers to her dad as Joel. It reminds her of Lauren calling her mom Tibou.

"How so?"

"Well, you're naturally angry at Joel about us—about him and me—and for breaking up his marriage with your mom, but now that you've gone and broken some rules, you have that in common."

Carly hasn't thought of it this way.

"You're saying that now that I've messed up my own life, I should be more understanding of my father messing up his?"

"Something like that. But I wouldn't put the emphasis on messing up."

"It's kind of hard to get away from that when you've been lying and faking who you are and . . . and in my case, failing out of school and getting expelled."

"Well, when you put it that way," Edwin says, and takes a drag on his cigarette.

"Are you gonna go parental on me, or can I have one of those?"

"I'm not your parent." Edwin takes a cigarette from the pack in his breast pocket, lights it from his own, and hands it to Carly. "I look at lives in a more forgiving way. Those things you did are done for a reason, not for the bad results you happened to have gotten."

Carly drags deeply on her cigarette and blows the smoke up toward the ceiling.

"Yeah, well, when someone shoots a person dead, it's called murder, whether you meant it or not."

"Whoa! Hold on here, Carly. No one has been shot, and no one's dead."

As Carly thinks this over, her gaze wanders around the room and settles on the painting with the big black streak across the canvas.

"Has Joel gotten over his abstraction being violated by that hippie painter who came to sign it?"

Carly uses the index and middle fingers on both hands to make air quotes around the word "abstraction." She likes the way it feels—modern and grown-up—calling her dad Joel.

"Oh, right, he went ballistic over that. It took a while, but I talked him down from a major lawsuit. Only kidding. I think Joel's grown to like it that way. He's actually considering buying another Brian Waterfall."

Edwin makes the same gesture Carly made and puts air quotes around the painter's name as he pronounces it.

"He's gotten to be a very big deal in art circles. I personally have little use for his work," Edwin adds, and blows a string of smoke rings toward the painting. "In fact, I'm strictly a figurative guy. I like pictures that look like what they're supposed to be."

"Me too," Carly chimes in, delighted with what Edwin is saying. "I like paintings of people and landscapes and still lifes."

"Right. Solid stuff you can trust. That's what's wanted, not all that scribble scrabble."

She and Edwin are still laughing when Carly hears a key turn in the door, and Joel comes in and greets them.

"Hi, guys. Sorry to be late. Someone got pushed onto the tracks at Columbus Circle, and the whole West Side subway is shut down. Nightmare! I walked twenty blocks before I could catch a cab."

"Were they killed?" Carly asks.

"They didn't release any more information, but it's hard to survive being run over by a train."

Edwin catches Carly's eye and shakes his head slowly. "Now, that's messed up!"

"Feet, Carly," Joel says. "Off the cocktail table, please."

"Function doesn't always follow form," Edwin explains, and winks at Carly. "Joel's look-alike Giacometti is intended more as art object than footstool."

"I see that I'm outnumbered in my own home," Joel complains as he pours himself a glass of iced tea.

Carly likes the way Edwin and Joel tease each other but obviously get along. She tries to remember but can't come up with an example of when her mother and father ever acted like this.

She has been dreading a soppy T-group session with her father and Edwin explaining and defending their relationship, but the evening goes much differently than expected. Edwin spent the afternoon shopping at the mega Fairway on 125th and the river, and he proudly sets out ingredients for a Thai stir-fry, naming them one by one as he places them on the counter.

"Vidalias," he says, and plunks down two large onions the size of softballs. "Carrots. Peppers. Porcini and fiddlehead mushrooms. And . . ." Edwin digs into the vegetable drawer and pulls out a big bunch of something green. "Ta-da, cilantro!"

"Give us a break, Edwin," Joel says. "It's dinner we're putting on, not a theatrical production."

"But they're the same thing," Edwin whines as he runs a big knife through an electric sharpener set by the stove. "Here, Carly, you can perform the honors."

"Of killing someone?" she kids.

Edwin laughs. "Of chopping vegetables while I prepare the rice and sauce."

"How about me?" Joel pouts. "Don't I get an assignment?"

"You get to set the table and open the wine."

The dinner is delicious, and Carly asks for seconds.

"The shrimp is great," Joel says as he helps her to a heaping scoop.

"Citarella," Edwin says. "Fairway's good for the other stuff, but Citarella can't be beat for fresh seafood."

"Good job," Joel says, nodding his head approvingly and smiling at Edwin.

Carly imagines one of her father's ads with two gay guys playing house together. She gets the impression that Edwin's like the wife who does the cooking and that Joel gets to play the role of husband. Seeing it's almost ten o'clock, Carly announces that she'd better be heading home.

"I'll walk you to Broadway to get a cab," Joel says, grabbing his coat and keys. "It's impossible to get one on Riverside or West End at this hour."

On their way to Broadway, Joel tells her, "Edwin and I are looking into a bike trip on Nova Scotia over the summer. We'd love it if you'd come with us."

"The Lenskys have invited me to Vermont for a month." Carly has been looking forward to this for weeks now, and the thought of missing even part of the time she's scheduled to be with Lauren and hang out with her family is unbearable.

"That's great. How about if you reciprocate by asking Lauren to come with us on the bike trip, either before or after your month with her family?"

"Really?"

"Here, I got this for you." Joel hands her a brochure. "Look it over and see what you think."

"You got it for me?" Carly asks. She doesn't know why, but suddenly she's feeling weak, and her eyes are filling with tears. "I mean . . . I don't need to return it?"

"We've got another one. I ordered two. Show yours to Lauren."

"How come you're being so nice to me after I fucked up so badly?"

"Let's see," Joel says, and starts counting off reasons on his fingers: "Because you're human? Because we all fuck up? Because I love you? Oh, I know why! Because whale watching. We get to take a cruise and see migrating whales!"

"Awesome," Carly tells him. "I'll ask Lauren."

Joel hails a passing cab and hands her a five-dollar bill.

"Get home safely, sweetheart."

"Love you, Dad."

CHAPTER
THIRTY

To pack for her summer away, Carly works from lists posted on the mirror over her dresser. Gwen is helping her make piles of stuff to choose from, and then Carly's going to make the final cut when she gets everything laid out.

The packing is complicated by the bike trip to Nova Scotia, which is scheduled at the end of the month Carly will be spending in Vermont with the Lenskys. Joel and Edwin are driving from New York and picking up her and Lauren on the way.

"It's overwhelming," Carly complains. "How the hell can I know what the weather will be?"

"August up north can get chilly, especially the nights," Gwen offers. "Best to be on the safe side and prepare for a combination of hot and cold. You should probably throw in rain gear too, just in case."

"I don't suppose the bike tour has laundry facilities?" Carly muses.

"Think camping trip, even though you'll be staying in B&B's. Here's that list from the tour operators of things you'll need."

Carly takes the page Gwen hands her and marches over to her bedroom mirror, but it's already covered with lists and Post-its.

Gwen pulls a piece of tape off the dispenser on Carly's desk. "Tape it to the wall next to the mirror, why not?"

Carly takes the tape from Gwen's thumb, sticks it on the list, and then hesitates before taping it to the wall.

"What about the paint? Won't the tape make it peel off?"

"We're due for a paint job," Gwen says. "If I can ever get organized enough around here to get to it."

Carly can't help noticing how much Gwen has eased up about all the stuff she used to be fanatical about.

Gwen goes back over to the bed and picks up a dark green hoodie with white lettering on the back.

"I like this new sweatshirt from Allendale. Why not pack it with some nylon turtlenecks? Layering's always a good way to hedge your bets with weather."

"I think I'll save it for when I start school," Carly tells her mother. "I'll take my old navy-blue one instead."

In the spring when Carly visited the Allendale School in Bucks County, Pennsylvania, she felt comfortable right away on the large, leafy campus. Kids were lying around on the grass and playing Frisbee between classes. She even felt good in the headmaster's office, where a litter of shar-pei pups was scrambling around and making little noises in a basket by his desk. At one point in their interview the headmaster, Mr. McAdams, buzzed his secretary and asked her to bring in "Charlotte." Carly wondered if Charlotte was another girl applying to the school, but then the secretary came in with the full-grown mother shar-pei so the babies could nurse.

"Lunchtime at the pound," Mr. McAdams said with a smile, and then asked Carly, "Do you have any pets?"

"Uh, well, w-we live in New York City in an apartment," Carly stammered. "My parents always said we didn't have enough room for pets."

"Another good reason to come to school in the country. If you'd like, when they're finished nursing, you could handle the pups. They're very friendly. Just be careful they don't pee on you."

Carly laughed and told Mr. McAdams, "I love shar-peis. They're so cute and crinkly."

The rest of the interview was a breeze. Carly figured that anyone who could talk about puppies peeing on you couldn't be too judgmental about anything she might say. The kids at Allendale were nice, too, and acted friendly in the class Carly attended and in the cafeteria where she had lunch.

Carly especially likes that Allendale has a reputation for being less competitive and grade obsessed than a lot of other places. Plus, it's coed. It felt cool being in a school where guys and girls all hang out together. And since they don't have uniforms, the kids were mostly wearing jeans and sneakers, with a few who even braved the early spring chill in shorts and T-shirts. Carly's eager to tell Lauren all about it so she'll know that now Carly can wear normal clothes to school too.

Carly was upset at first that she'd be repeating junior year, but Allendale has a system of mixed grades, where kids take courses according to their level of advancement. It turns out that even though she'll technically be in eleventh grade, Carly's essay on *Tess of the d'Urbervilles*, which she submitted as part of her application, earned her a place in a twelfth-grade writing course.

It's already evening by the time Carly and Gwen finish Carly's packing. The big beige duffel bag sits at the foot of Carly's bed, stuffed so full that the zipper won't close.

"Shall we?" Gwen says as she kicks off her slippers and places a bare foot on top of the duffel.

"Go for it," Carly says, and jumps on the other end of the bag.

The two of them convulse in giddy laughter while they jump up and down on the overstuffed duffel.

Carly can barely catch her breath when she stops for a moment, holding herself steady to dispel the dizzy feeling. "I need to go pee," she says.

"I think I already have," Gwen says, and they convulse in laughter again before Carly leaves the room.

As Carly sets about straightening up and putting away the clothes she has decided not to pack, she comes across her Serena wig, stuffed in a corner of the bottom dresser drawer. She hasn't thought about the wig for a long time, and now it feels startling and a little scary, as though there's a ghost of another person in the room.

At first Carly takes it out, thinking of trying it on again, just to see the way she looked as Serena. But a wave of fear and revulsion overcomes her and makes her stop before she lifts the long, black, wavy locks to her head. Instead, she begins to stuff the wig back in the drawer, but then she gets another idea. She lays it on her bed and roots around for a piece of paper to wrap it in. When she's done wrapping the wig, Carly writes a note and tapes it to the package:

Dear Susan,

I'm off for the summer and then to boarding school in Pennsylvania in the fall, so I won't be working on the children's floor again. Please see that some little girl like Germaine, who lost her hair from chemo treatments for her leukemia, gets this wig. Thanks for letting me help out. I loved being with the kids and seeing how much fun they could still have, even though they were very sick. Take care and keep up the great work!

Love, Carly

It's late now, with only enough light in the sky for Carly to make out the shapes of the buildings along the West Side skyline, etched in violet shadow above the Reservoir, which has turned a shimmering gold. Sunsets make her think of Daniel with sadness and regret. Not to see one speck of the world, not one rising sun or one that sets. She remembers the last time she left his apartment and the miserable night she spent that ended her pregnancy and nearly cost her her life.

Carly shuts down these thoughts and writes another ending to the story. She pictures herself with Daniel one more time, wishing him well with his Fulbright and the future. She imagines him being kind to her and gentle, the way he was when she liked him best, at the beginning when things were fun and everything felt new and exciting. She imagines him saying her real name, Carly, for the first time, and maybe even telling her he loves her, that he always has and always will, and kissing her goodbye and wishing her good luck.

Then Carly thinks about how hard it will be for Daniel to get around in an entirely new environment like the one he'll be moving to when he goes on his fellowship to Germany. She imagines him changing his mind and deciding not to leave and maybe even asking her to come back to him.

But Carly knows there's a difference between a story that's real and one that's make-believe. Even if she can make choices about the story she writes for herself, she can't control Daniel's story. She knows that he will wind up doing what he wants to do, which is to go away, like Hamlet should have done, and start a fresh chapter of his life, like she's about to start with her own life.

Carly goes over to her squashed-down duffel bag and manages to zip it up. It makes a soft ledge for her to sit on while she turns her thoughts to the good stuff that's happening. Lately,

Carly has been feeling grateful: for the new school she'll be going to in the fall, for the month she'll be spending at the Lenskys' in Vermont and the bike trip on Nova Scotia with Joel and Edwin, for her mother's understanding and forgiveness.

Looking out across Central Park just in time to catch the sky emblazoned with light from the setting sun, she suddenly feels glad for something else, something she used to resent but which has come to feel much better. Now she's glad to be Carly Klein.

ACKNOWLEDGMENTS

owe special thanks to dear friends Cathy Birkhahn, Ann Marks, Jan Saks, and Rosalie Siegel, who read early drafts and provided support and encouragement. Thanks, too, goes to independent editor John Paine, who understood where I wanted to go and helped focus the manuscript. And I'm abundantly grateful to Brooke Warner and Shannon Green at She Writes Press and SparkPress for favoring *Becoming Carly Klein* with their faith and hard work.

ABOUT THE AUTHOR

Photo credit: Kevin Gordon

Elizabeth Harlan grew up and went to high school and college in New York City, where her story is set. She has written young adult novels and a literary biography for adult readers. Her recurring theme is mother/daughter relationships. Having mothered two children and grandmothered four grandchildren, she still identifies most powerfully with young girls struggling to grow out from under the oppressive yolk of misguided mothering. She lives on the East End of Long Island and on a barrier island off the West Coast of Florida.

Looking for your next great read?

We can help!

Visit www.gosparkpress.com/next-read
or scan the QR code below for a list
of our recommended titles.

SparkPress is an independent boutique publisher
delivering high-quality, entertaining, and engaging
content that enhances readers' lives, with a special
focus on commercial and genre fiction.